I0557439

RED RIVER STATION

Westerman Tales

WILLIAM BURGDORF

Copyright © 2018 William Burgdorf

ISBN-13: 978-09989320-6-4

Book design by Champagne Book Design

www.waburgdorf.com

BOOKS BY
WILLIAM BURGDORF

The Bierman Saga

The New Mexican

Company A

The Arizonan

Humps and Hooves

DEDICATION

Jesse Chisholm's wagon trail from his trading post, near present day Wichita, Kansas, stretched two hundred and twenty miles into Indian Territory for trading purposes. It ultimately was utilized as a significant portion of the cattle highway that ran, in its heyday, from San Antonio, Texas, to Abilene, Kansas. From the first herd to travel north in 1867 until 1884 when barbed wire, the Kansas quarantine laws, and relocation of the railhead ended the drives, approximately five million head of cattle, and a million mustangs traveled the Chisholm Trail. It was the greatest migration of livestock in world history.

This book is dedicated to the cowboys who braved the elements of nature, catastrophes, man-made devilment, and bull-headed beeves as they rode into history.

I also dedicate this story to Nancy. Without her continued support and editing, this tale would never be told.

1

GATHERING

THE MORNING SUN BREAKS OVER THE RUGGED landscape of rolling hills speckled with scrub brush and cacti. Rocky outcroppings cut by arroyos and gullies are washed by past torrential rains.

In the clear, crisp, cold morning air, the short Mexican boy races in pursuit. He knows it's an important race. An escape for freedom. His rapid breathing creates puffs of frost. The white cotton pullover and baggy *pantalones* flap about his spindly body.

The runaway goat zigs and zags as it dashes along the steep path dodging prickly pear cacti. His breakaway run for freedom moves down the trail away from the village.

The boy's shouts and threats are choked back as he slides to a stop at the end of the draw. Before him stands a motionless rider astride a tall buckskin. The fifteen-hands-high horse's neck skin quivers in a spot an insect bites, but the horse remains still.

The rider sits with one boot in a stirrup, and his other leg is wrapped around the saddle horn. His well-worn boots dangle on the same side of the horse. The boy watches the rider's head turn toward him. From under the dust-covered, wide-brimmed, tall-crowned hat, two piercing smoky gray eyes probe the short Mexican boy's own wide-open, ebony eyes.

"*Perdón, Señor.* I did not know you are here."

"'Pears you're havin' goat trouble."

"*Si, si, mi cabrillo*, kid, *es muy importante* to *mi familia.*"

The rider shifts his chaps-covered leg from around the saddle horn, placing it back into its stirrup. He unties his lariat, takes the rope, dallies one end around the saddle horn, shakes it out, and begins twirling a slow rolling loop over his head with his left hand. The boy watches in amazement as the loop grows in size. Suddenly, the rider rises, stands in his stirrups, and with a deft flick of his left hand, sails the rope and loop through the air. Lazily, it drifts and undulates as if alive. It settles around the head of the runaway goat. The rope snaps taut.

The goat is lifted from its feet and dumped onto its back, bleating as if shot. The animal thrashes around, struggling to regain a standing position.

The Mexican boy rushes to the downed goat, quickly ties a lead rope around its neck, undoes the lariat, and tosses it aside. The rider pulls the lariat back to him, recoils it, and attaches it to his saddle.

"*Gracias, Señor.*" The boy firmly grips the lead rope while the goat tugs to get away.

"*Da nada,* little friend."

"*Comprende*, I appreciate your catching *mi cabrillo*. How can I help you?"

The rider leans forward, his leather vest gaps open revealing a holstered Colt Peacemaker buckled around his waist. His red plaid shirt is dusty from miles covered on horseback. The steely eyes bore into the boy's face.

"You seen any other Gringos around here?"

Chadbourne Westerman stretches his twenty-four-year-old body to unkink stiff muscles as he rides away from the Mexican boy's village.

I've been straddlin' this saddle for a spell. Uvalde is some ways behind me, and Fredericksburg should be along directly.

Removing his hat, he runs his hand through his long brown hair.

The herd is only a few miles ahead of me now.

Weaving his way through the dense growth of prickly pear, dwarf oak, catclaw, and bois d'arc hedgerows, he once again finds the wide trail left by the cattle.

Mister McCray put me on this path when he found his son hanging from the oak tree on his ranch. The boy was roundin' up cattle to throw in on the drive north. His Pa hired me to find out who killed him. I'd have done it for nothin'. I sure liked that boy. He was a good sort. Hard workin' and wantin' to learn everything about bein' a cowman. It was a vile lowlife that killed him. I'll find 'em and settle the score. That boy deserved better than to end his life like that.

Riding up to the top of a draw, Chad spots the village of Fredericksburg. A gathering of wood framed buildings along the main street is surrounded by multistoried homes scattered in every direction.

Hard to believe that I found two more dead boys between Uvalde and here. One tied up by his hands and danglin' from a Cottonwood tree, horsewhipped to death, and the other lyin' beside the trail with his throat slashed.

Chad wonders what else the trail will reveal as his horse walks down the hill toward town.

Tonight's a good meal and soft bed. The herd has to cross the Pedernales River, so I can catch up tomorrow. Who's killin' these boys and why? Most of these cowboys are only fifteen to twenty-one, and the average trail boss ain't no more than twenty-five to thirty. Didn't figure bein' a range detective would lead to trailin' death like this.

From within a bois d'arc hedgerow, black, hooded, vacant eyes carefully search the gathering cattle.

Trail herds from ranches in the hill country have been collecting together to form a drive to the Red River and north on the Chisholm Trail to Abilene, Kansas.

The serpent-like eyes roam over the riders as if devouring each one its gaze rests upon.

Chad slowly approaches the livery in Fredericksburg and dismounts.

"Hello, anybody here?"

From inside the barn he hears, "Hold your horses, I'm

comin." With a limp, a skinny stable hand shuffles to the livery doorway. "All right, all right. Whatcha want?"

"Friend, I need a good rubdown for my horse along with a bucket of oats. Can you manage that?"

"If I can't, I imagine I better look for some other kind of work. You here for a spell?"

"Nope. Ridin' out tomorrow morning. I figure you see almost everyone who comes into town don't you?"

"I reckon I see a right smart many of them. Why?"

"You see any stranger lately? Anyone who seems on the run or anxious to get in and out of town?"

"You mean anyone besides yourself?" asks the stable hand.

With a smirk, Chad replies, "Yeah, besides me."

"I know'd most everybody here about, but yesterday a feller did stop by. He watered his horse, and I got him stabled. It's that gray over in the end stall."

Chad looks down the line of eight stalls, half of them occupied, and spots the gray.

"You mind if I take a look at the horse?"

"Suit yourself, mister. Its owner didn't tell me to keep him a secret."

"Obliged. Sorry about your leg."

"Ain't nothin', friend. Throw'd while breakin' broncs, landed wrong, and busted my leg. Never healed right, but I manage."

"That you do. Yep, that you do. I'll take a look at that horse." Chad moves to the stall and checks out the gray. He pats the horse's withers, rubs its muzzle, and looks for obvious marks of having been ridden hard. Nothing out of the ordinary, he decides. He walks back to the barn doorway and the stable hand.

"See what you wanted?" asks the liveryman.

"More like didn't see anything unexpected," answers Chad.

5

"You know where the jasper went who owns the horse?"

"Where's anybody go who's been saddle bound for a while? He went over to the Frisco saloon beside the hotel. It's down the street. Look over yonder, you can see it."

Chad looks up the street and spots the saloon. "Thanks. I'll head that way myself. Treat my horse like family, okay?"

"Always do. Don't intend to change now," says the stable hand as he leads Chad's horse into the livery.

Store fronts line both sides of the street Chad walks along. He stops to look at hand tools, buckets of nails, and cooking utensils in the front window of the General Store. Next is a dress shop with blue and red fabric displayed in their window. He crosses the muddy street and steps on the wood sidewalk in front of a barber shop. He sees the barber shaving a client laid back in the swivel chair. With a flick of a raised straight razor, the barber gives a quick wave to Chad. Chad nods back. In the road, buckboards rattle past loaded with ranch supplies and cowboys plod their ponies down Main Street. The scent of fresh-baked bread smacks Chad in the face causing his stomach to growl as he walks past a bakery. Passing four more buildings, he comes to the Frisco.

With the late afternoon sun warming his back, Chad drapes his arms over the batwing doors of the saloon. His eyes adjust to the dark interior as he scans the space. On the left side, ten tables are scattered around, each surrounded by straight-backed chairs. By the front door a Faro dealer lazily flops cards on the game board waiting for gamblers to arrive. The bar tender busily washes glasses and lines them up along the bar top that stretches along the right side of the room. At the bar stands a middle-aged man with salt and pepper hair, cowboy hat pushed back on his head, holstered Colt buckled about his waist, and sipping slowly on a foamy glass of beer. Chad shoves the door open and walks toward the bar.

"I'll take a glass of what he's drinkin'," says Chad indicating the middle-aged man.

"Howdy, stranger. Passin' through?" asks the Colt-toting man at the bar.

"Could be," says Chad. He nods thanks to the bartender as a beer is set in front of him.

"Let's be clear," says the man pulling his vest back to reveal a star pinned to his shirtpocket. "Passin' through or what?"

"Sheriff, you're just the man I want to see," says Chad. "I'm Chadbourne Westerman from down Uvalde way."

"I don't care if you're Sam damned Houston. You still haven't answered my question."

"I'm a range detective trailin' a killer. He may be in your town, and I need your help," says Chad.

"You have a mighty convoluted way of answering my simple question. Why should I help you? You got any kind of credentials that shows you're a detective, or am I just supposed to take your word?"

"I've got a letter from the Cattleman's Association of Castroville employing me as their range detective." He reaches into his vest pocket and takes out an oilskin-covered packet. Opening it, he extracts the letter and hands it to the sheriff.

After reviewing the document, the sheriff hands it back. "Okay, so you're a range detective. A mite off your range, ain't you?"

"Well, that depends, sheriff. I'm trackin' a killer and go

where he goes."

"Think he's around here?"

"Could be."

"So, how can I help?"

"Was hopin' for that."

"Say your piece then."

"Any strangers been around town in the last few days?"

"Folks come and go. Can't say that any real strangers lingered."

"Anybody seem like they weren't too partial to seein' you or being sociable?"

"No, not so I can recall. Wait. There's one fella. Ran into him last night. Tall, slinky, didn't look me in the eye, seemed kinda weaselly."

"He still in town?"

"Believe so. Try the hotel or boardin' house. Wait…Hell, he's probably down to Madame Kate's."

"An eatin' joint?"

"Not by a long sight."

"What then?"

"A whore house, end of the street, out of town by about fifty yards. You can't miss it. Two stories and all bright pink."

"I'll find it."

"I reckon so. Kate's shines for miles on a sunny day." The sheriff smiles.

"Thanks, sheriff. I'll look for an out of towner there. He, by chance, leave any name?"

"None that I recall. He did wear a long black duster. Didn't take it off. Strange."

"Here's for another beer, sheriff. I appreciate your help." Chad slaps two bits on the bar and slowly walks out of the saloon.

Chadbourne raps on the paint chipped front door of Kate's. He waits patiently and then knocks again, harder this time.

"Yeah, yeah, I heard you the first time," says a voice from behind the door as it's yanked open. Chad takes a step backwards as a full-sized woman stuffed in a green dressing gown stands in the doorway. The gown gaps open at the top and almost fails to restrain her large breasts that bulge the fabric as if trying to escape.

Chad stares at the woman's breasts but her shocking red hair distracts his attention. However, no amount of rouge can conceal the lines and creases at her eyes, mouth, and forehead.

"We ain't open yet," she says as she moves to slam the door.

Chad shoves his boot between the door and frame.

"Get away from my door," yells the woman. "I'll send for the Sheriff, and he'll fix you. He ought to. I pay him enough."

"I ain't a regular payin' customer. The Sheriff sent me this direction. I am payin' for information." Chad lifts a silver dollar from his vest pocket and flips it through the air toward the woman.

With snake-like reflexes, she snatches the coin out of the air and deposits it in her ample cleavage.

"Okay, ask your question, cowboy."

"I'm trackin' a fellar. Tall. Slinky. Wears a black duster. Has he been here?"

"You find that scum, you beat him within an inch of his worthless life, cowboy. He stopped here, got interested in Fannie Lorelai. She's one of my girls, a sweet girl who wouldn't hurt a fly. That monster commenced to beatin' her. I kicked in the door to her room when I heard her screaming, and he lit out the window."

"How long ago? Have any idea where he went?"

"If he were here I'd have twisted his damn head off by now. He went out the window heading for town. You find him, you beat him."

"I'll try to find him, ma'am." Chad yanks his foot from the doorway and hurries toward town. He slows long enough to look in the saloon and then heads directly toward the livery stable.

"Hello; you hidin' out?" Chad shouts. No response from inside. He walks into the barn and immediately notices the gray horse is gone. He hears a groan from the stall. Running to the opening, he sees the liveryman lying on the ground holding his head. Blood seeps between his fingers.

Chad kneels down. "Easy, easy, don't move around too much. Anything broken? Can you see anything? What happened?"

The liveryman moves around and slowly sits up. The left side of his head is smeared with blood.

"He pistol-whipped me. The miserable damned son-of-a-bitch slipped up behind me and slammed his pistol against my head. I guess he figured to kill me."

"How long ago?"

"Hell, he cold-cocked me. I don't know. An hour or two, maybe."

"Is my horse ready to go?"

"Sure, sure. Help me up so I can get my feet under me."

Standing, Chad says, "Here, lean on me. Ease yourself up. You want me to send for the doctor?"

"Cowboy, don't worry the doctor. I'm the best liniment

pusher this town's got." The stableman stands.

"I got to get after him. You'll be all right?"

"Sure, sure. Go get the SOB and square things up for me. Go on."

Chad rushes to the stall holding his horse, saddles him, mounts, and spurs his way out of town. He figures his prey left directly from the livery end of town instead of racing down Main Street.

A few minutes on the road reveals where hoof prints dug in deep and churned up the dirt.

Someone is heading out of town in a hurry. Got to get my man. I got to keep from losing his trail among all the other prints on this road.

2

MAKING COWBOYS

THE SHALLOW VALLEY BETWEEN ROWS OF ROLLING hills is filled with milling cattle. It's been a hard ride from Fredericksburg. Chad knows his horse needs a rest. The trail he's followed has been swallowed up in other hoof prints on the road.

He sits with his leg wrapped around the saddle horn to steady himself while rolling a smoke. He shakes out loose tobacco from a Bull Durham pouch onto the piece of paper pinched between his fingers. Grabbing the loose strings with his teeth, he tugs closed the pouch and places it back in his vest pocket. He licks the edge of the cigarette paper and rolls it together. Pulling a Lucifer from his other vest pocket, he strikes it on the handle of his pistol, and he lights the cigarette, inhales deeply, and slowly exhales a plume of smoke. His gaze watches cowboys riding among the cattle, harassing them into some semblance of a herd. He notices two riders break away from the work and trot up the hillside toward him.

"Well, I can't believe my eyes. Angus Tremain, is that you?" shouts Chad as the men draw closer. "Who's that taggin' along with you? Russell Thomas, what are you doin' here?"

"Chadbourne Westerman, what hole did you crawl out of?" asks Angus. "We're supposed to be here, but you're a long way from Uvalde."

"Ain't that the truth. I'm a lot farther than I'd like to be. That's for sure."

Both riders pull to a stop facing Chad and lean over their saddle horns, crossing their arms on their horse's necks.

"You lost or lookin' for a job?" Angus asks.

"Truth is, boys, I'm a range detective now and chasing a killer."

"Get out of here," says Russell. "The last time we was together, you was top hand down on Mister McCray's spread. You give up the good life?"

"McCray is to blame for me being here. He got me papers to be a detective and put me on the trail to find his son's killer."

"You don't say." Angus sits up straight and pushes his hat back on his head. "Come on over to the chuckwagon so we can get the whole story. I got Manolito Tito cookin' for us on this drive. You remember him, don't you?"

"You bet. That man can throw the best biscuits anybody ever laid their lips around. What he does with coffee is almost sinful. Best brew I ever had."

"Wagon's on the other side of the herd." Angus takes off his hat, runs a hand through his brown hair, replaces his hat, and tugs it down tight on his head.

The three men ride through the milling cattle, stop their horses, dismount, and find a log beside the campfire to sit on. The chuckwagon is close to a stone-rimmed fire circle. Piled up beside the wagon are a dozen bedrolls waiting for their owners to claim. The cook stirs the bed of coals in the fire, making room to set a Dutch oven. He returns to the open shelf on the end of the wagon and continues working with a pair of ceramic bowls.

"You said McCray's boy was killed?" asks Russell.

"He found the boy hung from an oak tree. It was a real sad day for us all."

"Any idea who done it?"

"Nothin' around to show who, what, or why. That's when he said he'd hire me, get me papers, and expect me to find out what happened to his boy. So, here I am."

"Damn, that's a charge you've got to keep," Russell replies.

"A couple of days later, I found a boy hung up by his hands from a cottonwood and beat to death, and another one beside the trail with his throat cut. Different herds. Different locations. It appears, they were all heading here."

"You mean, the boys were drivin' their cattle to join up with us?"

"Can't be certain, but it appears to be that. Rustlin' wasn't the object because their cattle were just wanderin' around, scattered from one valley to another," says Chad.

"Well, if that don't beat all. Any leads on a killer?" Angus asks.

"Thought I was on to one in Fredericksburg but lost the trail. All I know is he was heading this way." He watches Angus for his reaction.

From under his black Stetson, Angus stares at Chad, and

with a steady, unwavering voice says, "Whoever it is better not be dogging my drive. I've been charged to lead this outfit to Abilene, and by the Almighty, that's where we're goin'."

Chad smirks, and replies, "Angus, you weren't shy of eighteen and ridin' drag the first time you went up the trail in '65. The second time, in '67, you were top hand and ridin' point. And now, in '71, at all of twenty-four, you're trail bossin'. I've known you since you were mutton bustin' sheep on your *Abuelo's ranchero* in the Nueces Strip. Your Granddaddy sold horses to my Pa to start our herd. All I'm sayin' is watch your back. Somethin' evil's sniffin' around this drive."

"What evil? We've got some meaner than snakes Longhorns down there," says Angus.

"Russ, you ain't as old as Angus. I wonder what you're doin' here," Chad says.

"Angus talked me into running his remuda for this drive."

"I reckon you know more about horses than any other two people I know. Seems like he made a good choice, makin' you wrangler."

"Oh hell, cut the sweet talkin', Chad. I already told Angus I'd get his horses to Abilene and him back to Texas."

Taking off his hat and running his hand through his hair, Angus says, "Thanks for the warning, Chad. You and me have sat around many a campfire. I've got families driving their cattle to me to make up a marketable herd. I expect to have twenty-five hundred head come the end of the week.

"That's a lot of beef, Angus," says Chad.

"These families are trustin' me to take their cattle to Abilene and sell them for top dollar. I've got to pick a dozen boys from all those you see with their cattle in the valley, make cowboys out of them, take 'em up the trail, and bring them back home to their mamas. I aim to do that or die tryin'."

"I know you take it serious, Angus. Do you mind if I tag along, kind of keepin' an eye on what's happenin' around the herd? I ain't drawin' wages or workin' for you, already got an employer. I just want to get to the bottom of the killings."

"You know, I could use another top hand."

"Not interested this time, Angus. Is that a 'yes' to my shadowing your herd?"

"Sure. Do what you need to do. In the meantime, I've got cattle to brand, cowboys to grow, and a herd of the orneriest longhorns the good Lord ever created to wrestle all the way to Kansas. If you ladies will stop jaw-jackin' with me, I gotta go to work." He dusts his hat against his chaps, slaps it on his head, rises, mounts his sorrel, and rides toward the cattle. Russ is right behind.

The ebony eyes follow Angus, Russ, and Chad while they talk and then go their separate ways.

The morning sun creeps over the horizon. Chad awakes to hear horses snorting and stirring around. The sound of whooping and hollering comes from a circle of boys standing near the remuda. Chad rolls up his bedroll, tosses it toward the chuckwagon, moves toward the coffee pot that's keeping warm beside the fire, pours a cup, and moves to join the gathering.

In the center of the circle, a horse rears, jumps, bows its back, and comes down stiff-legged as it attempts to dislodge the rider on its back. More whoops, shouts, and hurrahs.

"Hang tight."

"Don't get throwed."

Two boys slap each other on the back.

"Grab a handful of mane and hang on."

"Don't let that little horse scare you any."

A short boy grabs his hat and waves it up and down.

"Ride 'em."

Chad watches the animal buck, twist, turn, and thrash its way around the circle intent on ridding itself of its passenger. Suddenly, the saddle empties as the boy flies through the air and tumbles onto the ground. The horse kicks its hind legs high as if to say, *I've shown you.*

Outside the circle, Chad sees two young boys sitting on the ground resting their heads on their knees. He spots Russell standing toward the back of the crowd and walks up to him.

"Looks like a couple hit hard and still feel the effects."

Russell keeps his eyes on the circle. "They'll shake it off and be good as new, shortly."

"So, Angus is separatin' the wheat from the chaff?"

"All a boy's got to do is stay three minutes on ol' Catamount." Russell squints into the dust being raised by the horse.

"You pick the horse, or did Angus?"

"Well, he asked my opinion, and Catamount's about the most unrideable horse I know."

"You have any that stick for three minutes yet?"

"There are two of them so far. Only got ten more to go," replies Russell.

Chad watches Angus pull the lariat around the fifteen-hands-high strawberry roan stallion's neck. He takes a couple of wraps around a young elm tree he's using as a snubbing post.

Jerking the horse's head close to the tree, he quickly ties his bandana across the halter covering the horse's eyes, grabs an ear, and yanks on it drawing the horse's head down.

Another boy dressed in dusty Levis, a gray bib-front shirt, and a sweat stained wide-brimmed hat, jumps up into the stirrup. He throws his leg over the horse, settles into the saddle, yanks his hat down tight on his head, grabs a handful of halter rope, and nods.

"Hang on, Benjamin," shouts a boy from the circle.

"It's only got to be three minutes," a short boy hollers.

Angus yanks off the bandana and releases the lariat.

Catamount springs into the air, lands with a bone-jarring impact, commencing to buck and twist.

The boys roar, shouting encouragement for both rider and horse.

"YeeeHaww, ride 'em."

"Pitch him Catamount, toss that sorry excuse of a cowboy."

"Hang on. Get a grip."

"Ride' em."

After three minutes of punishment, the rider slides from the saddle onto the ground and quickly rolls away from the thrashing horse.

Two waiting boys yank the rider upright.

"You did it, Ben. You made the three minutes."

"You're lucky that mean thing didn't stove you up. You made it."

They pound congratulations on Benjamin's back as he stumbles to put distance between himself and Catamount.

"Looks like number three," says Chad.

"I believe that boy's a keeper," replies Russell.

"Ol' Catamount has more twists and turns than the Brazos."

"That he does. He can swap ends in the blink of an eye and leave whoever is on his back clawin' at air."

"Angus is havin' too much fun doin' this. I'm goin' over to see what Manolito's keepin' warm from breakfast. You comin'?"

"Naw, I've got to go with that boy." Russell nods toward the one who just completed his ride. "I need to help him rope the three mounts he wants for his string. Besides, I might find one or two of these cowboys that can help me with the remuda. You go ahead."

Chad ambles away from the noise and dust of the bronc riding to a quieter spot where Manolito has the chuckwagon set up.

"*Señor* Chad, it's good to see you again. It has been a long time, no?"

"Manolito, it's been way too long. You was busy last night so I didn't get a chance to talk with you. How's your family?"

"Ah, *mi espousa, hijo, y hija estás bueno, bueno*. I will miss them on this drive but need the job."

"Good to hear the family's well. Y'all got any spare saddle horns and coffee left from breakfast?"

"*Ay*, saddle horns is what you means as biscuits, *si*?"

"You're right, Manolito. Pitch me one."

"*Señor* Chad, you know I always keep coffee hot and plenty of biscuits." He hands a covered basket to Chad, who helps himself to a couple of the hot and flaky saddle horns.

"You wouldn't have a smidge of molasses stashed in a drawer on the wagon, would you? Sure would go right well with these belly warmers."

"*Señor,* your sweets tooths is still with you, *si*?" Manolito hands Chad a can he pulls from a drawer.

"*Muchas gracias, amigo*." Chad picks up a tin cup and

moves to the coffee pot on the campfire. Settling himself on a rock, he begins sipping the coffee and taking a bite of his biscuit. Another loud roar rises from the boys.

"Ride 'em, Slim."

"Stick tight."

"Don't let go."

"Pitch 'em, Catamount. Pitch 'em"

First step is to make sure they can stick to a horse. It's an old lesson that all boys need to learn. Next, Angus will get them ropin', cuttin' out cattle, and stayin' in the saddle all day. It's the only way to turn boys into cowboys. Some will even be men by the time the drive ends. Chad smiles as he pours molasses on his biscuit.

Damn, another hole. This road is rutted so bad it's almost impassable. Whatever has walked over it has the dirt churned up and almost impossible to drive over. Isaac Wisenheimer's wagon jolts along the roadway leaving Fredericksburg. His twenty-year-old body bounces on the seat with every bump. A black flat-crowned hat tries to control his wavy brown hair. He tries to straighten the creases of his pinned striped trousers, tugs at his black vest, and brushes trail dust from the sleeves of his not so white shirt. *It was nothing short of a miracle to get safely out of Comfort. That damned fool filled the gate of my wagon with buckshot. Better it than me. I didn't tell him the formula was a sure cure for gout, but did he listen? No. What does he expect for a dollar…miraculous healing?*

Isaac's two horses steadily plod along tugging his home on wheels behind them. The wagon is short bedded with sideboards and a solid top. A hinged platform on one side drops down to form a stage. Inside are all the worldly items needed to live: clothing, cooking utensils, even a rocking chair, and five cases of Dr. Isaac Wisenheimer's Tonic. The wagon jolts along as the horses, without guidance from the driver, resolutely move down the road. The sign board attached to the side of the wagon reads:

Dr. Isaac Wisenheimer
—Pharmacist—Restorative tonics—
—Cures for Ailments, Rheumatism, Colic, and Lumbago—
Feeling Tired and Rundown? Dr. Wisenheimer has the cure.

I know the good folks in Bastrop told me not to go to Comfort, but those Germans have money. It was too good to pass up. Besides, I sold a case of tonic, which should hold me a week or so. The sheriff in Fredericksburg wouldn't even let me set up shop before he hustled me out of town. What is all that caterwauling up ahead?

The noise in front of him causes him to rein in his horses and stand to get a better look. In the valley stretches a mass of cattle. Horsemen ride around and through the herd. Everyone is busy and pay him no attention. He spots a lone rider descending from a hill and approaching his wagon.

"Howdy," says the rider. "Hope you ain't in any hurry."

"I'll have you know that I am," replies Isaac. "Do you own those cattle?"

"No. They're owned by a bunch of folks around here and being gathered for a drive to the north."

"Who can I talk to about clearing a way for me to pass, I'm on business."

"I can give you the name of the man you want to talk to,

even better, point him out to you, but it ain't goin' to do any good to ask."

"And why is that, good sir?"

"Because he ain't gonna do it."

"See here. I'm a citizen and demand to have a right of way."

"Well, friend, you can demand all you want, but Angus ain't gonna give you no never mind."

"Just who are you to tell me that, sir?"

"Name's Chadbourne Westerman. I suppose I'm talkin' to Dr. Isaac Wisenheimer, if I'm reading the name on the sideboard of your wagon correctly."

"You are, and yes, I am Dr. Isaac Wisenheimer."

"A real honest to goodness doctor?"

"My good man, I've studied with the finest teachers in the art and science of pharmaceutical compilations, and the dispensing of viscous formulas for the containment and correction of a multiplicity of ailments and injuries. My title as doctor is an earned one over years of practical application. Does that response enlighten you and address your inquiry?"

"Yep. You're a snake oil salesman."

"How dare you impugn my dignity and denigrate my occupation with so vile and slanderous a term."

"How you do spin words. How long can you keep goin' without repeating yourself?"

"My good man, kindly clear away so I can continue my journey." Isaac flicks the reins of his team.

Chad reaches over and grabs a handful of the reins.

"Whoa, friend. No need to get everything in a twist. You can't go bustin' into that herd without causing damage to them and you. Turn your team and follow me. We'll ease over toward where the chuckwagon is staked out."

"Indeed. Just why would I willingly follow you?"

"Because that's where the grub and coffee are."

When was the last time I ate? Yesterday? Could it have been day before? Coffee and food, I'll follow this cowboy.

"Lead on, my good man. Let's see what epicurean delights await us at the dining parlor you've described."

"Angus will have a cow when he hears you," says Chad with a grin.

Arriving at the chuckwagon, he helps Isaac unhitch his horses, hobble them, and turn them out to graze.

"Manolito, this here is Dr. Isaac Wisenheimer." Chad introduces the two men.

"My pleasure, sir," says Isaac extending his right hand.

"*Mucho gusto, señor,*" replies Manolito grasping the offered handshake. "What can I do for you gentlemens."

"We'd be obliged for some of your fine coffee," answers Chad. He sits on a log by the smoldering campfire. "Grab a seat, Isaac. I'd like to know more about what you're doin' out here." Chad pats a spot on the log.

Using his handkerchief, Isaac brushes away the dirt. "I find myself between towns at the present time. The authorities in Fredericksburg were rather brisk with me, and I'm en route to the next major town. Which one would that be?"

"Heading this direction, I reckon your next fair size town will be Llano. It ain't much more that a frontier trading center with a few log buildings housing business establishments, a post office, and some homes. Though it does serve the farmers and ranchers around it."

"Splendid. In a burg of that nature, I should be able to encourage an audience for the pharmaceutical goods I offer."

"If you mean that snake oil you're peddlin', I'd say you'll find yourself strung up mighty quick."

"Sir, must you continue to denigrate my profession? While I accept your hospitality, I find your derogatory nature stifling. Is there any food available here?"

With a laugh, Chad motions to Manolito to bring something to eat and receives a nod in reply.

"Isaac, you fling those words around slicker than a polecat slidin' on an iced over pond. I do need to ask you some important questions."

"Very well, go ahead."

"You said you left Fredericksburg. Right?"

"Assuredly."

"Did anyone pass you on the road? Someone in a big hurry?"

"The byway was somewhat travelled. Two, they appeared to be buffalo hunters, passed en route headed to Fredericksburg. A wagon loaded with farm implements overtook me and proceeded down the road. My team caught up with and passed a nun riding a donkey. Strange, she did not have an escort. One rider on a gray horse did gallop past me. I would not have given it any thought except for the black duster. It streamed out behind him, flapping almost like a flag."

"Did it appear the rider was heading this way?"

"I don't know. Once the horse sped past, I lost attention and frankly, don't know which direction he went."

"I'm tracking a killer, and that might have been my man. You know, the weirdest idea just came to me. Where are you eventually headin'?"

"No particular destination is currently in my mind. I fancy that I'll go where the wind blows me."

"Great. How about if it blows you to Abilene, Kansas?"

"Why, in all of creation, would I want to go there?"

"'Cause that's where this herd is goin', and I'm thinkin' I can use your assistance in running a killer to ground. You've seen him, and he's seen you. If nothin' else, you're good bait."

"Now, just a minute. I have no intention of being used to lure some malcontent or miscreant to you."

"So you'd rather be out on the prairie, by yourself and have the mis..miscre..miscreature slip up and cut your throat?"

Grabbing his own throat, Isaac looks at Chad in alarm. "Surely, that would never happen, would it?"

"You saw him, and he saw you. What do you think?"

"Good, sir…"

"Will you quit callin' me that? My name's Chad. Get used to it. Think about this. I'm sure there are those in the towns you've left in a hurry who'd love to know where you are. I imagine there might even be an interested lawman. What do you think?"

"I think your subject is becoming boring and tiresome." Isaac fidgets and looks nervously around the campsite.

What if he does let those malcontents know where I am? There are at least two marshals interested in my whereabouts.

"The way I see it," says Chad, "We have an opportunity to help each other. I don't give you up, and you help me solve my mystery. Life's too short to be on the dodge, so are you willing to help me?"

"Have you left me an option?"

"Nope. It's all or none. Your choice."

"It appears that I'll assist you in your endeavor for the time being."

"Great." Chad slaps his hand against his leg. "We've got a distance to go together. By the way, what's in that tonic you sell?"

Reaching into his hip pocket, Isaac extracts a flask. Patting it he says, "This, my friend, is the finest combination of complementary ingredients designed and concocted to provide relief from the plethora of ills and aches that plague mankind."

"Let me see it." Chad grabs the flask from Isaac, opens it, and takes a mouthful. He swishes the liquid around in his mouth and spits it into the fire. A brilliant blue flame erupts from the embers and quickly burns out.

Licking his lips, Chad pauses a moment, then says, "I taste Old Grand Dad, a touch of turpentine or liniment or both, and, let's see, yep, it's got cayenne pepper. Did you put gunpowder in it, too? Just how far off am I, Isaac?" He hands the flask back to Wisenheimer.

"You know that you are making it exceedingly difficult to like you, don't you?" Isaac replaces the flask into his hip pocket as he glares at Chad.

"Like me or not, you're stuck with me, and I'm stuck with you until we find out who or what was on that gray horse. You're the one on borrowed time, Isaac."

"You've made your point, Mr. Westerman. It appears that I'm your reluctant accomplice although I don't know how I can help you."

"We'll find a way, Isaac. We'll find a way even if I have to make a cowboy out of you."

"Oh, good Lord. Anything but one of those ruffians."

Manolito walks over and offers plates of frijoles and tortillas along with two tin cups. "The coffee, shes be ready *un momento.*"

Isaac ignominiously slurps the beans from the plate and sops up the juice with his tortilla.

Chad gestures toward Isaac and laughs.

"Manolito. I believe he likes your cookin.'"

3

HEAD 'EM UP, MOVE' EM OUT

I<small>T'S EARLY, C</small>HAD HEARS THE CATTLE MILLING AROUND. Daylight creases the ridges to the east and begins to filter across the prairie. He rises in the predawn morning to see four young boys loading bedrolls and saddlebags on their horses.

"Gettin' an early start?" Chad scratches his head and runs his hand over his beard stubbled face.

"Yes, sir," says a brown-haired boy with a hint of a lisp. "Mr. Tremain made his choice for trail hands. He says, "We," the boy points at the other three, "are still a little young. He'll take us next year. He did pay us for our time, and we appreciate that."

"Angus is good for his word, boys. He'll do what he says. You're headin' home then?"

"Yes, sir. All of us got long rides ahead of us."

"Well, good luck. By the way, what's your name?"

"I'm Samuel Roberts, sir. Over there is the Menger twins, Slim and Bob, they're headin' for Fredericksburg. Ron Keeping is riding with them goin' home to Blanco, and I'm riding by myself to Fort Mason."

"Ride safe, boys." Chad pats the rump of the Roberts boy's horse. The boys all nod, mount, pull their hats down tight, and ride away into the predawn.

Chad walks back to his bed and stretches out waiting for morning. Angus is letting the crew sleep in before the drive begins, knowing later on shut-eye may be something hard to come by.

Mid-morning, Chad gets up, rolls his bedding, and stashes it in Isaac's wagon. Isaac is still snoring. Walking to the campfire, he sees Angus stomping around, his face almost as red as the shirt he wears. The cowboys have finished breakfast, cleared out, and ridden to the herd. Chad sits on his heels, pours a cup of coffee and sips at it while watching Angus' temper go from bad to worse.

"Look," Angus finally bursts, "I said you could shadow the drive, but there wasn't nothin' said about a peddler's wagon taggin' along. Hell, all we need is a brass band, and we'd have an everlovin' parade," shouts Angus.

Chad stares at Angus. "Do you feel better? Are you about over throwin' your fit?" Chad takes another swig of coffee, certain that he has Angus' attention. "It's a wagon, and he'll follow with Manolito so's to not bother nobody. It ain't nothin' big, and he's probably a dead man if we turn him loose."

Angus snaps back, "You understand that you're responsible for him. If he gets in the way, he's gone. Got that? Gone. I don't care if whatever it is out there guts him and skins him. I've got a cattle drive to take care of, not some snake oil peddler."

"Just so you know, he takes real offense to that reference," says Chad.

Angus' face turns from red to crimson as his temper explodes.

"He takes offense, he takes offense…Oh, hell." Angus removes his hat and throws it to the ground. "Just keep him away from me." He sweeps his hat up, dust and all, shakes it off, and shoves it on his head. As he strides away, Angus kicks a sack of potatoes beside the chuckwagon, curses under his breath, reaches the picket line, unties his horse, mounts, and rides toward the herd.

"Well, that went well." Chad says aloud taking another sip of coffee.

I guess I better find Isaac and give him the rules. Angus is liable to strangle him and save whatever is out there the trouble.

Late morning, Isaac walks into the campfire circle with an armload of firewood muttering to himself.

"It has been ten days of waiting. Ten days. I could have been in - what is it? Llano. I could have established and reaped the rewards of honest work, sold tonics to cure the ill, made matronly women feel beautiful, males act stronger, and horses able to race from here to Kansas." He pulls a monogrammed handkerchief from his back pocket, shakes it open, and wipes his brow. "Instead, I am here performing manual labor and frittering away time."

"*Si, Señor* Isaac, we will have some *las fritters muy pronto* with the firewoods you gather," replies Manolito.

Isaac looks at Manolito and shakes his head.

"Quit bellyaching, Isaac," Chad lectures. "Angus is fixin' to get things moving. Just this morning he sent home the last four boys. Now, he has his trail crew of twelve riders – two point, two swing, two flankers, and four drag. He even kept two extra boys to help Russell with the remuda." Chad blows on his coffee and takes another swig. "In the past ten days, he's taught them boys to stick to their horses, rope, brand, chivvy cattle along, and work as a team. Everything else, they'll learn on the trail."

"Well, hoo-rah. I'm thrilled for them." Isaac dumps the wood in a pile by the campfire. "What did you say about fritters, Manolito?"

"*Si, Señor* Isaac, I makes *las fritters*. You will see, no?"

"The food is the only redeeming element of my sequester. Did you say four boys were sent home, Chad?"

"Yep, Angus only wants the best cowhands. He did pay those goin' home a week's wages, but they were disappointed havin' to leave."

"Didn't you say you found boys murdered on your way here?"

"Yep, sure did…Oh, hell. I should have warned those boys. I told them to ride safe but didn't tell them the danger. Grab a horse, we gotta go." Chad leaps up and races to the picket line for his horse.

"I don't have a horse," shouts Isaac.

Chad stops and spins around. "You can ride, can't you?"

"Well, of course, I can ride. I just don't have a horse."

"Come on, let's hustle over to the remuda. Russell can cut a horse out for you. Hurry."

Chad races to the horses as Isaac follows, spitting and sputtering.

Russell throws a lasso around the neck of a blaze-faced horse with four white stockings.

Borrowing a spare saddle, Isaac mounts. He holds a rein in each hand extended straight out about three feet apart.

"What in the blazes are you doing?" Chad asks.

"Preparing to ride. That's what."

"Just how are you fixin' to control a pony with the reins like you have them?"

"With ease and finesse."

"With what? Oh, hell, never mind. Just stick to the tail of my buckskin and don't get yourself lost."

"Do you know where those young cowboys went?"

"I know the two Menger boys were headed back towards Fredericksburg. The Keeping kid is ridin' with them before he turns southeast toward Blanco. We're going after the Roberts boy. He's by himself, headin' west toward Fort Mason. Let's go."

Chad spurs his buckskin into a full gallop, glances over his shoulder, and spots Isaac bouncing along in pursuit. By late afternoon, they cover fifteen miles of rolling hills covered with scrub brush and stunted trees. Alternating between walking and galloping, Chad suddenly calls a halt. Up ahead he spots birds circling overhead.

"Damn, double damn, come on Isaac keep up." Chad spurs his buckskin over the next hill. Dropping down into the shallow valley, he sees a horse standing still with its reins dragging the ground. A figure is stretched out beside the animal. Galloping up, Chad springs from his horse and crouches beside the body.

Isaac rides up and sees the young boy spread-eagled, naked, and staked out on the ground. His clothes are carefully rolled up and stacked on top of his boots beside the horse. The boy's body is split from crotch to ribcage. Blood, gore, and entrails are pulled out and strewn around. Isaac sees shock and horror in the glassy-eyed stare of the boy. He leans over and vomits the contents of his stomach.

"When you're done heavin' up your socks, get down and find something to dig with," says Chad. "We can't leave him like this. Let's get him buried before dark."

Climbing down from his horse, wiping his mouth with the back of his hand, Isaac asks, "Who would do something like this?"

"It ain't Indians," says Chad. "Whoever did this is riding a horse that's shod." He dismounts and walks around the murder scene. He pulls a small notebook and a stubby pencil from his shirt pocket. He points at the ground around the body, makes notes, and sticks the notebook back into his pocket. "It's the same killer that murdered the others."

"How can you be sure?"

"The victims are young boys, they're involved with our herd, and the fiend is hangin' around lookin' for opportunity to catch them alone."

"Who or what is it?"

"If I knew that, you'd be on your way peddlin' more tonic."

"Do you think this could have happened to me?" asks Isaac.

"This poor boy may have paid the price for your reminder."

"Don't throw this child's death on me."

"I'm not, Isaac. You need to keep in mind what or who we're dealin' with. I need your help to end it. Are we together on this?"

"There may have been some resistance on my part before, but from this moment on, we are aligned."

"Good. Let's finish burying the Roberts boy, cover the grave with stone from that dry creek bed, and get back to the herd. Angus needs to know what's goin' on. It's gonna make things different."

They finish burying the body and ride back toward the herd. Chad leads the boy's horse.

I'll find you, and when I do, everything you did to these boys is gonna be visited on you. You can't hide from me forever. There ain't enough prairie for that.

Angus stomps around the campfire frustrated with the conversation. Chad watches his face turn a rosy shade of pink. "I know you told me about a killer you're chasing, but you didn't say nothin' about him stalkin' this herd? Do you hear what you're sayin'?" Angus shouts. "That's loco crazy talk. Why would anybody stalk a herd? I'm movin' these cattle out of here in the morning. We've got over seven hundred miles to cover. God knows how many creeks and rivers to cross, Indian Territory to get through, and now, a killer. Lordy, this just keeps gettin' better and better."

"You know you've got to double up on the night hawking, don't you?" asks Chad.

"Yeah, yeah. That makes sense. Glad I kept a couple of extra boys that tried out for the trail crew. All right, we are where we are. Damn shame about the Roberts kid, he was a real good sort. I ain't goin' to enjoy writin' the letter." He was a hard worker and tried hard to join this drive. He'd have growed up to be a good cowboy."

"He would have at that," says Chad, looking at the ground.

"Tomorrow morning, we leave. Manolito's already got the

tongue of the chuckwagon pointin' at the North Star and he'll do that every night for the drive. Get some sleep. I'll double the watch." Angus hangs his head and walks away from the fire.

Chad walks from the campfire looking for Isaac. He finds him sitting on the ground beside his wagon. "We got our work cut out for us," Chad remarks solemnly. "Gotta find that killer before something else happens. Once the herd moves, it'll string out for a few miles. The killer might think the pickin's easier and make a mistake. You want to put a cowboy drivin' your wagon and ride with me, or follow along behind Manolito?"

"I think I'll handle my wagon for a day or so as we get started. I can always get someone to drive it later." Isaac winces as he stands and rubs his saddle sores. "I'm turning in, I've seen enough today, and morning is going to come early."

"It'll be a plumb chuck full day, too." Chad says.

The sun peeks over the horizon as the lowing, bawling cattle stir and mill around on a flat stretch of praire. The cowboys whistle, shout, and crowd the animals onto their feet and form them into a drive herd. The point drovers prod the lead steer to move along the trail. As it steps out, the other cattle fall into line. Angus sits on his horse in front of the moving herd watching it come to life. Gradually, steadily the mass of beef moves itself northward.

Chad is comfortably astride his horse beside Isaac's wagon. "There you have it, Isaac. It's a sight to behold. Twenty-five hundred head of cattle on the move. This herd is gonna stretch for a good two miles. Watch the swing and flank riders. They'll try to form the herd up into walking three or four abreast."

"Look at the dust they are kicking up." Isaac shakes out his now dingy monogrammed handkerchief and covers his nose and mouth. "There is no hiding this herd is there?"

"Nope. Just be glad you're not ridin' drag. Those four boys on the downwind side of this mess of longhorns will eat dust from here to Kansas, not to mention gettin' blistered faces and hands."

"Blisters?" asks Isaac.

"Yep, from body heat given off by the cattle. It's scorchin'."

"What are they dragging?"

"Drag means bringin' up the rear. They prod along the sick, lame, and lazy animals that constantly drop back. Most long-horns pick a position in a drive and keep it, a few push to the front and others fall back. Those boys are goin' to see the same cows from here to Kansas."

"How fast will we move?"

"With any luck they'll cover ten to twelve miles a day."

"What about calves that are born along the way?"

"Well, that's where it gets a little unpleasant for the boys ridin' drag."

"How much more unpleasant can it be than covered in dirt, blistered, and bored to death?" Isaac wrinkles his nose to sneeze.

"When cows calve, the drag rider needs to kill the calf and prod the mother back into the herd."

"That's beastly. Why would they do that? That calf is valuable."

"Yes and no. The herd has to move. Any one, man or beast, that can't keep up is eliminated: sick, lame, or newborn. There's no way to take care of a calf, and leaving it to the wilds of nature sure ain't right. It's a job that has to be done."

"And these boys do that?"

"These boys will be made men in short order. You grow up quick on the trail. There ain't any other choice."

"Cowboys. That's a term that I don't think I'll ever understand. They may be boys now, but grow to manhood soon, by necessity. Their world is life or death, and there is little or nothing in between, is there?"

"I think you've summed it up, Isaac. These cowboys will learn fast or be left behind. There's no option."

"All you and I have to do is keep them alive long enough to make that journey, right?"

"That's the plan," agrees Chad. "Let's go to Kansas." He spurs his horse to move forward with the herd. Isaac pockets his handkerchief and snaps the reins over his wagon's team as he moves in beside Manolito's chuck wagon.

As the dust cloud of the moving cattle rises over the south Texas prairie, a telescope is collapsed as its user slides back from the crest of the hill. Rising, the observer places the scope in a carrying case, puts it in a saddlebag, steps into the saddle, and slowly follows the herd.

4

FOLLOWED

THE WIND BLOWS ACROSS THE ROLLING HILLS, stirring the belly-deep-to-a-horse grass into undulating waves. Lying on the crest of a hill mashing down the grass around him, a man adjusts the focus of a telescope.

"What's it look like, Rafe?" asks the scraggly bearded rider sitting on his horse in the shallow valley behind the man. "How many trail hands they got?"

"Enough, Leroy, enough. It looks like there're a dozen and some." Rafe scratches his armpit attempting to catch the crawling critters there. A filthy black duster covers his worn-out boots, dirty Levis, and stained leather shirt. He wears a dirty gray cavalry hat with tarnished gold tassels. "Go get Raylin and Rooster. They should be five or six miles back. They're supposed to have some grub, and I'm hungry."

"You know that Raylin and Rooster don't like to be crowded along, don't you? And Rooster is plumb loco, thinks he's a chicken and crows all the time. Something just ain't right with that boy."

"Yeah, I know, but Raylin keeps him in line. Go on. When y'all git back, we'll figure on what to do with that herd. Git, ya hear?"

"I'm goin'." Leroy rides slowly away, cresting a hill and disappearing from view.

Rafe leans forward resting his crossed arms on his horse's neck.

I've got a moron, Leroy, an idiot in Rooster, and a heartless killer with Raylin. How did I end up here? I should be home in Nacogdoches, slopping pigs or choppin' cotton. This ain't the picture I'd painted in my mind when I shot that nosy, busy-body sheriff. Hell of a way to live. Oh, well, what's done is done. I've got cowboys to kill and cattle to steal. Rafe straightens, yanks his horse's reins to turn him around, and begins paralleling the herd's dust cloud.

Angus moves to the campfire and picks up the coffee pot. "Got the first real test comin' tomorrow morning, Chad. Puttin' the herd across the Colorado River below where the Llano ties on to it."

"I imagine that's so."

"Yes, sir. Tomorrow we separate the men from the boys."

"You know, you seem just plain happy to be pushin' your crew as well as the cattle." Chad throws the last dregs of his coffee into the fire. "I believe they'll fool you and do just fine."

"We'll find out. The nighthawks are ridin' around the herd, singing soft-like to keep everything settled down. Come dawn, we'll put the chuckwagon and your snake oil peddler's wagon across. Give them a head start. Then push the bell steer into the river for a swim."

"Do you know if all the boys can swim?"

"Can't say I do, but I guess after tomorrow if they don't, they will."

"Yep. You're one hard-nosed trail boss. I'll hang back and keep an eye out to see if anyone has trouble, if that's all right with you?"

"Fine by me. Remember, you don't work for me. I'm checking the herd before I turn in." Angus sloshes his remaining coffee into the fire and drops the tin cup in Manolito's tub of soapy water. He pauses to look around the camp, then walks to the picket line. Untying his horse, he mounts, and rides into the darkness.

Chad sits by the fire, and smirks. *I wonder who's gonna give in first, Angus or his crew? This is gonna be a real experience to see both parties learn a bunch.*

Rising, he walks over to Isaac's wagon, reaches in, and pulls out his bedroll. Isaac doesn't break rhythm as he continues to snore. Chad flips his blankets underneath the wagon, sits, pulls off his boots, and stretches out. Sleep comes easy.

Early in the morning, before the herd was brought up to the river, Manolito and Isaac move their wagons to the crossing. Manolito snaps the reins over his horses' backs, breaking them into a trot. They enter the water and quickly make their way across. The wagon floats momentarily and trails behind the team up the river bank to solid ground. Manolito stops his team and jumps to the ground. He walks back to help Isaac.

Isaac watches the crossing and moves his team into position. Standing on the driver's seat, Isaac gathers the reins into his hands.

"No, *señor*. Aiyyy, no," shouts Manolito. "Sit down, *por favor*. Do not stand like that."

"I can see better, Manolito. It is a better vantage point standing like this," Isaac shouts.

"No, *señor*. You will no cross the river like that. You will be in the river, *pronto*."

"This is the way charioteers drove their teams in history."

"I no care about cherry ears, *amigo*. I care about you not drowning. *Por favor, señor*, sit down."

"Very well. It just seems so plebian to drive in this manner."

"*Si, si, señor*. It is as you say pleeby. That is good, yes? You will live, no?"

"Yes, no. You do have a way of confusing me Manolito. At any rate, here we go."

Isaac snaps the reins over his team and they plunge into the river. Reaching midway, the wagon begins drifting downstream with the current.

"Now, *señor,* now, snaps the reins," shouts Manolito.

Isaac cracks the reins and the horses pull through the water and climb the bank.

"Well, that was not that difficult. In fact, it was quite exhilarating."

"*Si, señor*, that is what I think also." Manolito climbs back onto his wagon seat shaking his head. *Caramba,* **él** *est uno loco Gringo.*

Chad sits to the side of the herd. He's been watching the preparation to cross since sun up. He sees the drag riders start pushing the herd toward the river. Swing riders and flanker cowboys hold them together and bunched up. The cattle object by vocalizing their discomfort, huffing, puffing, and mooing. Once the bell steer is in the water and moving, the pressure from the rear of the herd forces the main group to follow. The point riders splash back and forth across the river helping move cattle through the water.

The bellowing and lowing is constant and along with that noise, Chad hears the crashing, clashing, and grinding of horns as the cattle thrash around getting stable footing. He knows the greatest danger, besides drowning, is for an unexpected head toss, spearing a cowboy's horse or the rider. Longhorn cattle have perfected using their horns for defense. Years of running wild have taught them how to impale bothersome creatures with a quick twist of their head. Being in the water, flailing around, is a recipe for disaster.

"Hold 'em, hold 'em, hold 'em," Angus shouts over the cattle, bellowing and objecting to entering the water. "Catch that bunch drifting your way, Shorty." Angus points at three cows drifting downstream toward the drag rider sitting on his horse in mid-river. The water washes over his saddle up to his waist and the horse's neck. The cowboy wears only long johns.

Reluctant cattle keep stumbling down the bank and entering the water. At mid-river, the bell steer appears to have second thoughts and starts to turn around.

Angus twists around in his saddle and points toward the

steer. "Git him, git him, Bob. Don't let him turn. Straighten that critter out."

Chad watches a skinny, freckle-faced cowboy ride quickly into the river and drop a lariat over the bell steer's horns. He moves out front and pulls the steer's head around, pointing it toward the far bank. Slowly, loudly, the animal begins plodding, floating, and swimming across. Cattle follow, and soon the steer gets his footing and climbs the far bank.

Bob shakes his rope loose, turns around, and heads back into the water looking for another cow to get across.

Steadily, the herd continues to plunge into the water. They splash around, some float, most swim across as they drift somewhat downstream with the current. Drag riders catch those unable to escape the current and push them to shore.

The sun is well up. Chad takes off his hat and wipes his brow with his forearm. Looking into the sky, he judges it's about midafternoon.

Not bad timing for gettin' the better part of twenty-five hundred cattle to the other side of a major river. Looks like only about two hundred or so left to cross.

He knows that on the other side, the cattle are being allowed to graze and recover from the crossing. Also, Manolito has his chuckwagon set up to prepare an evening meal.

I got no idea what Isaac is doing, but hope he stays out of Angus' way. 'Bout time to cross over.

Chad rides upstream of the herd and finds an easy crossing. Guiding his horse carefully down the bank, they slip into the water. His boots hang around his neck, tied together with a piggin' string. His clothes, firearms, sleeping roll, and saddlebags went with Isaac's wagon. He's riding in long johns like the cowboys and pulls his hat tight down on his head.

The last bunch of cattle approach the river and splash their way toward deep water. Drag rider, Benjamin Johns, is pushing them along. At mid-river, four cows break from the herd and try to return to the shore they left behind. Benjamin urges his horse to cut them off and force them across.

Chad watches from his swimming horse to see how Benjamin handles the breakaway cattle.

In a sudden move, one longhorn lunges toward Benjamin's horse. The cowboy deftly moves his mount away from the cow's twisting head. The current continues to drift the cows, and a sudden lunge by the larger cow nicks the horse with the end of a horn. In wild-eyed terror, the horse rears. Benjamin is thrown into the river, and the cattle lumber toward the downed rider.

Knowing the outcome can't be good, Chad drops his boots around his horse's neck and leaves his saddle, swimming quickly toward the floundering cowboy. He slips between the cattle, grabs the collar of the boy's long johns. Reaching out, he hangs on to the cow's horn. Their weight forces the cow to turn around and move across the river.

Nearing shore, Chad releases his hold on the cow, pushes himself away from the staggering animal, climbing up the bank. He draws the boy to him and shoves him into shallow water.

Benjamin stands and reaches out, grabbing Chad's hand and pulling him to his feet. "Sure am glad you saw me."

"Lucky to be there." Chad stands and releases his grip on Benjamin's hand. "I've had something like that happen to me a while ago."

"I feel dumb as a post getting tossed like that."

"Ain't been a cowboy yet who hasn't been unhorsed a few times."

"You ain't gonna spread it around are you, mister?"

"Not my story to tell, cowboy. You better go claim your horse before anyone gets any wiser."

"Yes, sir. Thanks again. I'm obliged."

"No thanks necessary. Just learn from it, and don't get your horse betwixt those longhorns again."

"I'll pay particular attention." The cowboy shakes water from himself and sloshes up the bank.

Angus sits on his horse beside Chad's mount. Looking at the river crossing, he watches the last cows climb out of the water. On top of the hill behind them he spots a horseback figure in a long coat.

Chad turns around, looking for his mount. He spots him upriver on the bank, foraging on river grass. Chad climbs the bank and walks toward Angus.

"You don't work for me. Is that right?" asks Angus.

"Yep. Don't work for you."

"Then what are you doing rescuing my drownin' cowboys?"

"Seemed like the mannerly thing to do at the time."

"It did, did it?"

"Yep. Otherwise you'd be havin' to write his momma a letter, and I ain't that sure you can write."

"I can write just as good as you, and you know it."

"Yeah, but spellin' ain't your strong suit."

"That might be, but seein' things is. What do you make of

that jasper watchin' us from the hill back a ways?"

"I saw him a while ago. He been there long?"

"Long enough to see us cross the last bunch."

"You gonna check him out?"

"Hell, no. I've got cattle to drive. I thought you was the detective," Angus says with a grin. "Go detect."

"I imagine I'll wait a bit to see if he crosses over after us. That okay with you?"

"Suit yourself. Just find out and let me know. Are you finished prancing around in your long johns now?"

"Well, I ain't real partial to bein' a red target for a long rifle from a hilltop, if that's what you mean."

"I reckon."

"I believe I'll get mounted and collect my gear from Isaac's wagon. After you bed the herd, I'll circle back." Chad gathers his reins and steps into his saddle. He pauses to pour water from his boots still hanging from his saddle. "Damn hard on boots, getting them soaked."

"Yeah. They'll dry. You'll dry. Let's move. Cows can't wait." Angus turns toward the disappearing cattle. "Oh, thanks for pullin' out the Johns kid. He's a keeper, and his family is good people."

"That's what us detectives do, Angus. We take care of things."

Angus shakes his head and spurs his horse into a gallop.

The suppertime coffee pot is making its way around the circle of cowboys for a third time. Chad sits wondering about the rider on the hill. *Why would someone watch the herd? Who is it? Is he alone? This is going to take some investigating.*

Chad stands and hands his empty cup to Isaac.

"I'm goin' to ride back a ways to check on some things. Anybody asks about me, tell them I'll be back directly."

"You need anybody to ride with you?"

"Nope. I want to go nice and quiet like."

"So," Isaac scoffs. "I'm too noisy to ride with?"

Chad shrugs. "Ain't so much the noise, just the continuous conversating."

"Well, excuse me, but conversation is the civilized way to deport oneself."

"Yep, but conversating when it ain't necessary is also liable to get a man killed."

"Have it your way. I'll let interested others know your return is imminent."

"Yep. You do just that…imminent. Sometimes, I think you just make up words."

"I'll have you know…"

"Just let them know I'll be…imminent. Okay?"

Isaac nods. "Good."

Chad mounts his horse and quietly rides away from the herd retracing their route to the river. As he approaches the river, he rides up a hill and dismounts. Ground tying his horse, he crouches and creeps to the crest. Lying on his belly, he scans the landscape for a tell-tale fire. He's rewarded with a faint flicker beside the river. It is partially obscured by a timber fall of driftwood washed downriver during a flood. Returning to his horse, he picks up the reins and slowly begins walking in the direction of the fire.

The campfire snaps and crackles, sending sparks into the night sky. Four men gather around the firepit.

"When do we do something, Rafe?" whines Leroy. "We been followin' along like you said. Ain't we goin' to take the herd?"

"Yeah. When, Rafe?" Raylin's shaggy mane of hair shakes as he nods his head. His Mexican serape stinks. A growth of black beard surrounds his lower face and a full moustache crowds his upper lip. Bushy eyebrows shade his eyes, making his head appear to be surrounded by a hairy mass. His foul breath from rotting teeth precedes his question. He's as large as a bear.

"I'm only goin' to tell y'all one more time. Listen, and listen good."

"I'm listenin', Rafe," whines Leroy.

Rooster sits, clucking softly. There's a glitter of madness in his eyes. His red hair is unkempt and rises in spikes on his head. A long neck is punctuated with a prominent Adam's Apple. His body is skinny to the point of emaciation. His disheveled appearance confirms he's more animal than man. Filthy rags of cast off clothing cover portions of his body. He reeks of excrement and sits in a squat with jerking movements of his head. His eyes constantly dart from left to right, missing nothing.

"What do y'all know about herding cattle?" asks Rafe. "Nothin', right? Well, why should we take the herd before they're driven to market? Let the cowboys do the work, and we hit them just before Abilene or wherever they're bound. Do you understand?"

"Sure, sure, Rafe. We understand." Leroy quickly looks at Raylin who slowly nods his head. "It's the waitin' that's hard. Most the time we just hit and run. This time is different."

"Yeah, it's different, but the payoff is a helluva lot more. So, we wait. You got it?"

Rooster stands, stretches his neck, and screeches out a terrifying crow. His hands are folded into his armpits and his arms flap like wings. He squats again.

Rafe glares at Raylin. "I told you to keep him quiet. Your idiot brother is goin' to get us killed." Rafe raises his hand to backhand Rooster who scuttles out of his reach.

"Shut up, moron. Shut up. I'm goin' to shoot you if you sound off again."

"You ain't shootin' my brother." Raylin moves his large body to a more comfortable position. "I said I'd take care of him. I will. You hurt him, I'll squash you."

"Yeah, yeah. Hard to do with a bullet rattlin' around in your head," says Rafe.

"You'll have to empty that six-shooter to stop me, and you ain't that quick." Raylin smiles a ferocious grin.

"Hey, hey, we're talkin' about cows," says Leroy trying to defuse an awkward situation.

"I'm goin' to check the horses," says Rafe, rising and walking away from the fire.

After Rafe walks away from the fire into the darkness, Raylin says, "I'm thinkin' I'm gonna pull his head offin' his shoulders."

"Not until we get them cattle sold. Once we get the money, I don't care what you do to him," says Leroy.

Rooster rises as if he intends to crow. He glances at Raylin who raises his hand, and he stifles the urge, clucking to himself instead.

Rafe stops at the horses and nuzzles the muzzle of his horse.

I'm going to kill every one of them. Not one will be missed, and I'll be doing the world a favor.

He walks away from the horses and unbuttoning his fly, relieves himself.

Only three feet away, Chad lies motionless, pulling up tight to the base of a mesquite bush.

I've had people trying to piss on me my entire life, but this is the closest its ever came to bein' real. Sounds like this bunch is ready to kill each other.

Chad sees Rafe button up, stand contemplating the night sky, walk back to the fire, and sit on his bedroll.

Easing away from the gang, Chad quietly returns to his horse. He takes the reins and slowly walks into the night.

A shadowy figure rises from the ground six feet from where Chad lay hidden. The ebony eyes glare toward the campfire taking in the men sitting around the flames.

They turn and follow Chad.

5

UNEXPECTED COMPANY

THE AFTERNOON SUN WARMS CHAD AS HE RIDES beside Isaac's wagon. The countryside seems to roll on before him. One hill after another all connected by scrub brush and clumps of trees. "The boys have managed the Guadalupe, Lampasas, and Brazos Rivers so far," he says. "We're closing in on Cleburne shortly. There anybody who knows about you in Cleburne?"

"No, I have not been in this part of the country before."

"I imagine Angus is going to cut the boys loose when we reach Cleburne for some yee-haw time."

"What kind of expression is yee-haw?"

"You've had the luxury of bouncing around that wagon seat. What if you were saddleback, covered with dirt, trail grime, and the trail boss says you've got some yee-haw time comin'.

Do you think you could figure that out?"

"All right, I believe I understand. What does this place have to offer?"

"Seventeen saloons and an honest sheriff. If you don't cause any trouble, you don't get any trouble in his town. Them that do will spend time in his jail instead of being pistol-whipped."

"So, better treatment for those who get out of line," sums up Isaac.

"Yep. The next stop up the trail is Fort Worth, and Angus isn't about to let his boys loose there. He'll probably drive the herd around town and only allow Manolito to go get supplies."

"Why not stop in Fort Worth?"

"Hell's Half Acre is why."

"Hell's what?"

"Part of downtown Fort Worth provides every vice a human can imagine: liquid, flesh, opium, and worse."

"Say, sounds like a place for my pharmaceutical miracles."

"Only if you don't intend to live long. There are sharpies in town who will see you comin' a mile away. They have a constabulary that's crooked as a dog's hind leg. If they catch on to you, you'll be lucky to leave with your life. Nope, Cleburne is the place to yee-haw, and then the next stop is Red River Station." Chad leans forward folding his arms and resting them on his horse's neck.

"So, I can set up shop when we get to town?"

"Nope. You can enjoy Cleburne."

"You do know you are making it extremely hard to like you, don't you?"

"Not in the likin' business. I'm in the keepin' y'all alive business."

"Well, for my money, you act as if every action taken is a life and death decision."

"That's the way it is on the frontier, Isaac. Things are life and death. Decisions made for you, or by you, can mean others or perhaps you yourself die, and not always quickly."

"You make it sound so dire."

"It is, and when we cross into Indian Territory, you might see just how cheap life really is. I hope not, but you may." Chad glances at the herd making its twelve-miles-a-day walk northward.

Cowboys surround the cattle and continue to chide them along by whistling, shouting, and slapping their hands against their chaps. The dust rises high in the sky over the animals, and he spots dirt-covered drag riders passing by Isaac's wagon on the hill. They wave and continue moving. The herd plods on.

"Where are we bound after Cleburne and Fort Worth?" Isaac waves back to the drag riders.

"We're about one hundred and fifty miles from the Red River. Angus will have to decide whether the best crossing is at Spanish Fort, Red River Station, or Colbert. It all depends on the herds in front of us and the cantankerous nature of the river."

"So, we are at least ten days to two weeks away from the Red River?"

"Kind of like that, yes." Chad watches the cattle move almost wave-like up one hill and down the other side.

"What do you mean by other herds?" asks Isaac.

"We're not the only outfit drivin' cattle to Abilene. There can be two, three, or more herds in front of us movin' north. You can see the trail we're followin' is pretty well stomped down. That means we've got company in front and probably other herds behind us."

"Angus is leading these twenty-five hundred head of cattle in this herd, and you are saying there is a high probability of other equally as large or larger herds being in front of us?"

"That's what I'm sayin'. Look at the trail. It's close to a quarter-mile wide. That means a bunch of lop-eared cows have travelled this way."

"Extrapolating a number then, that means there can be upwards of fifteen thousand cattle at the river. How can there be that many cattle in Texas?" Isaac's tone of voice is one of awe.

"Partner, we haven't begun to scratch the total of cattle in Texas. The more we push into Abilene, the more they want back East. The Chicago slaughter houses and meat packers can't process beef fast enough to satisfy the demand."

"I had no idea," says Isaac.

Chad realizes the magnitude of cattle moving north shocks Isaac. "We best move along to keep pace." He straightens up and lightly taps spurs to his mount.

Isaac snaps reins over his team.

They move forward.

Looking over his right shoulder, Chad views the endless stretch of rolling grass covered hills interspersed with islands of wooded groves.

On a distant hilltop, he spies a black silhouette, a lone mounted rider watching them.

Chad watches Angus direct the point riders to turn the herd and bed them down along the slow-flowing shallow Nolan River. While the cattle settle into place, he and Isaac arrive at the riverside camp set up by Manolito. Oak and cottonwood trees line the waterway, providing shelter, shade, and firewood.

The aroma of coffee fills the air, and Chad sees Manolito placing Dutch ovens in the coals, ready to receive the biscuit dough he pinches off and places in each one.

"I can smell your coffee a mile away," he says, tying his horse to the picket line that Manolito stakes out at every campsite. He walks over, grabs a tin cup from the chuckwagon, and helps himself to the fresh coffee.

"*Si, Señor* Chad. The coffee, she is ready. Biscuits be ready *muy pronto. Mi vaqueros* will be coming in soon for supper, no?"

"Has *Señor* Angus been by?"

"No, *amigo. Señor* Angus, he goes to town to make sure *el sheriff* knows we are here. *Es bueno*, no?"

"*Si*, Manolito. *Esta bueno* the sheriff knows. Although, I'm sure he's seen us comin' for a while. The dust cloud kicked up by the herd is hard to miss."

The cook busies himself preparing steaks and *frijoles*. Chad stands by the chuckwagon.

Isaac walks up, stretching his kinked muscles from the rough-riding wagon. "Coffee good?"

"Always is when Manolito makes it. Grab a cup and have some." Chad says.

"Not now. I noticed a lone rider trailed us this afternoon. Did you see that?"

"Saw that rider when we stopped aways back. I'm thinkin' we'll see more shortly. He might be coming in for coffee," Chad says with a chuckle. "Didn't appear to be more than one rider."

"That worry you?"

"Not yet. Need to see more to know more."

"I'll take that coffee now." Isaac rummages around on the chuckwagon tailgate and finds a clean cup. He steps to the coffeepot and pours a steaming cup of brew.

Both men watch as Manolito cooks up *frijoles*, steaks, and biscuits.

Cowboys begin riding in and tying up to the picket line. Washing away trail dirt in a basin beside the wagon, they grab a tin plate and extend it for Manolito to fill. Each moves to a spot beside the chuckwagon and sits cross-legged. They banter as they eat.

"Did you see that ol' mossy-horned steer make a move on me this afternoon?" asks a curly-haired cowboy.

"Yeah. He darn near hooked you, didn't he?" replies a freckle-faced drover.

"Gave it his best shot. My horse is smart and spun us out of the way just in time." Curly-hair feigns wiping sweat from his brow.

"Good that your horse is smarter than you are." An older boy butts into the conversation.

After finishing their meal, the cowboys walk to the shallow river, shed their clothes, and plunge into the water. Splashing and soaking, they scrub away the trail grit. Climbing onto the bank, the evening begins settling around them as they air dry before putting their clothes back on.

Birds and bats flit around the trees, hunting insects as the setting sun burns into the horizon.

Chad smiles. *I remember being just like them. With a full belly, smelling clean, still wet from a bath, and watching the day end. It's the best time for a drover. What does the lone rider want? Is he one of the gang that's tailing us? I'll need to talk with Angus.*

Angus slows his loping horse to a walk as he approaches camp. Dismounting, he ties the reins to the picket line, walks to the wagon, grabs a cup, and fills it with coffee. The Cowboys walk from the river and surround him.

"Who goes into town, Boss," asks Benjamin Johns. It's obvious the seventeen-year-old cowboy is anxious to visit Cleburne.

"Half the crew goes tonight and the other half tomorrow. Draw straws and make sure the herd is taken care of before anybody leaves."

"Anything we should know about town?" asks Benjamin.

"The sheriff is an obliging sort as long as nobody tries to bust up any establishments or hurrah any of his citizens." Angus looks at the other drovers gathered around and continues, "You do that, and you're in jail. Anybody in jail may just stay there. I'm not real inclined to bail you out, and if I do, any charges come out of your pay. Are we clear?"

The cowboys look at each other and nod in agreement.

"Is there a dance hall, Boss?" Benjamin looks at the other boys with a big grin on his face.

"Yes, son, there is, and the sheriff said folks are coming in tonight for a good ol' barn dance."

"Manolito, pull straws." Angus motions to the cook.

Manolito picks up a straw broom from his chuckwagon and snaps off a dozen bristles. He passes these to Angus who measures and snaps the straws into various lengths. Clutching the bundle of straws in his hand, Angus lets each boy draw a straw. "Short ones stay. Long ones go to town," he says.

Chad stands by the chuckwagon, watching the selection process.

Each boy draws a straw. Some smile and others stomp

away in disgust as they move toward the picket line to get mounted.

Benjamin turns around and almost collides with Chad.

"Doggone it. I don't get to go until tomorrow. What if all the good-looking girls don't stay over for the dance? What if the dance is only for tonight?"

"I believe you'll be just fine, son." Chad smiles at the young cowboy's impatience. "Mount up and go take care of the herd. Cleburne will be waitin' for you tomorrow." *You're only a young skinny sandy hair young man for a short time. I understand his disappointment. Patience is a skill that is hard to come by.*

Angus walks over to Chad and motions for him to step aside from the group. "You know you mentioned this drive's bein' stalked?" Pulling out cigarette paper and a pouch of tobacco from his vest pockets, Angus rolls a smoke, takes out a match, lights up, and inhales deeply.

"I know there's a gang of four riders that are shadowing this herd. They are lookin' to do something. Don't know when, but I don't imagine until Indian Territory."

"You're telling me this now? Why not the other night when you got back?" asks a sullen Angus.

"Didn't expect them to do anything sudden like. I'd imagine they are looking for the right time and place. By town isn't going to work for them."

"On my way to town, I came across a trail paralleling the herd. I back tracked it a ways. It's a single rider, stayin' low and out of sight. Didn't see who it was, but the trail was real clear, no attempt to hide it." Angus blows smoke rings as he exhales. "You think it might be one of the four you saw the other night?"

"Could be one of them is birddogging us until they make their move. Isaac and I also spotted a lone rider watching us late today."

"Lots of nosey folks out here," Angus says, "What about that killer?"

"We haven't seen anything since we buried the Roberts boy. It makes me kind of edgy not knowin' where, when, or if it's still out there. I'm not leaving this herd until I'm sure."

"You may want to take a ride at daylight toward town to make sure I saw that trail right. I'm doublin' the guard again while we're here just in case."

"That's a wise move. I'll check things out in the morning. What about our boys ridin' to and from town tonight?"

"I'll talk with them before they leave and tell them to stick together, not to leave anyone behind." Angus takes another deep drag on his cigarette.

"I'll make a circle of the herd with the nighthawks just to make sure everything's quiet."

"You don't work for me, you know."

"Yeah, yeah, I don't work for this sloppy outfit. I'm just out enjoyin' a ride. That okay by you?"

"Sure. It's a free country. Enjoy your ride." Angus crushes out the cigarette beneath his boot and walks toward the campfire.

Chad watches the boys heading for town grab their bedrolls and warbags from the chuckwagon and shake out some clean clothes to wear. He hears Isaac question Manolito about the ingredients in the peach cobbler he cooks in the Dutch oven.

The sun slides easily into the western horizon, and twilight settles as softly as a warm blanket around the outfit.

Chad listens to Angus wrap up his instructions to the

drovers headed for town.

"That's it boys. Everybody watches out for each other. Nobody leaves town alone. Y'all are back before sunup. Anybody that gets jailed, heaven help you because it'll be hell to pay when you're back here. Have fun. Now get before I change my mind."

Chad mounts up to ride around the herd.

Chad lies on his bedroll under Isaac's wagon listening to the mourning doves coo while daylight softens the eastern skies. Rays of sunlight begin streaking across the Texas prairie as morning explodes on the horizon. Rising, he quickly assembles his bedroll and tosses it into the wagon, waking Isaac in the process.

"It's early. Let me sleep," moans Isaac, rolling over as he returns to snoring.

Chad walks a short distance into the prairie, unhobbles his horse, and leads him down to the river. He returns to the wagon after the horse is watered and ties his mount to the tailgate. Manolito's coffee aroma catches his attention and he heads to the chuckwagon. Squatting beside the campfire, he grabs a waiting tin cup, fills it with java, takes a careful sip, and sighs with satisfaction.

"Manolito, your brew makes everything right with the world."

"*Si, Señor* Chad, and I thinks it tastes good too, no?" The cook hustles around the fire and chuckwagon preparing a fatback, biscuits, gravy, and *frijoles* breakfast for the trail crew.

"Yep, it tastes good, too. Did our boys make it back okay?"

"*Si, si.* They comes in late, late last night, or early this morning. I heard them and they all lined up to take the spoonsfuls of castor oil for the hangsovers."

With a quiet chuckle, Chad says, "That should bring them around right quick. *Señor* Angus been by yet?"

"Oh, *si, si. Señor* Angus is up before the sun and checking the herd."

Isaac stumbles to the chuckwagon half asleep, gropes for a cup, and feebly pours from the coffee pot.

"Why, in the name of all that's good, must the bunch of you begin your day at such an uncivilized hour? I should still be sleeping blissfully. The sun is barely over the horizon, boys are galloping around the herd, Manolito and you are chattering on about thus and such."

"Isaac, I do apologize for disturbing your slumber." Chad rolls his eyes and winks at Manolito. "Well, not really. Angus and the boys have a herd to babysit. Your comfort and convenience don't rightly figure into their plans. Sorry, pard, that's just the way it is."

"Are you going into Cleburne today?"

"Not right away. I'm going out to follow up on a trail Angus found yesterday. May be gone all morning or a mite longer."

"Well, let me know when you get back. I'd like to go into town and going with you is probably best. Manolito, biscuits, please amigo, biscuits." Isaac takes a plate of biscuits slathered with gravy and stumbles back to his wagon.

"I will let *Señor* Angus know you are checking things out, yes?" asks Manolito.

"You do that. I'll be back. *Gracias.*"

Chad saddles his horse, mounts, and rides east to locate the trail of the mysterious lone rider. It takes about an hour to arrive at the trail Angus discovered. It is clearly visible and there's been no attempt to hide it, as if the rider doesn't care about its discovery or not. Chad begins backtracking, moving slowly over the rolling hills and through the wooded areas always alert to his surroundings. Gently walking down an incline into another patch of oak trees, he is suddenly stunned as a low voice speaks.

"I heard you coming."

Twisting in the saddle, he grabs his pistol. Looking over his left shoulder, Chad sees a rider hidden in foliage and brush beside the trail. "Why are you hiding in there?"

"I didn't know who was coming, and I'm not about to wait in the open," the low voice answers.

"Well, get out here so I can see you," says Chad, turning his mount to face the hidden rider as he pulls his pistol from its holster.

With a rustle of brush and limbs, a mule moves into the open. Two ebony eyes peer back at him from a face surrounded by a white headpiece and a neck to shoulder covering. Over this is a black hood. The rider wears a black long sleeve dress. About the waist is a rope belt. Tucked under the belt is a strand of black beads with a crucifix hanging at the end.

Chad stares in amazement. *It's a…nun.* "What in the world are *you* doing out here?" he asks.

"Are you with the cattle drive?" the nun asks.

"Yes and no. You still haven't answered my question."

"I'm on my way to a mission in Indian Territory."

"That's all well and good, but where is your escort?"

"Don't need one."

"Why are you alone?"

"I'm never really alone." The nun holds up her crucifix.

"Do you realize the danger you face out here?"

"Nothing that the Lord cannot handle. My protection is stronger than anything that can come against me."

Astonished at the nun's response about being alone on the Texas prairie, Chad replies, "I know you believe that, and I'm not here to challenge you, but there are those who don't hold to that line of thinkin'. They'd just as soon be done with you and move on. You do realize the danger you're in, don't you?"

"My prayers have been answered. You have ridden to me."

"Whoa, just a minute. I'm nobody's answered prayer, but I will see you safe to the herd. From there the trail boss can decide what to do with you."

The ebony eyes don't flicker and continue to stare intensely at Chad. He involuntarily shivers under their gaze.

"Very well, let's go to the herd." The nun's low voice sounds like an order.

"First, who are you? Where are you from?"

"My name is Sister Maria from *Misión San Francisco de la Espada* in San Antonio."

"Sister Maria, I'm Chadbourne Westerman from Uvalde. Pleasure to make your acquaintance, but not under these circumstances."

"The pleasure is mine, Mister Westerman. Can we go to the herd now?"

"Follow me and stay close. It's not far."

"I know. I've followed you."

Chad leads the way toward the herd. His uneasiness doesn't leave him as he continues to wonder about the nun riding behind him.

Why would a nun travel like this?

I've known other nuns, but they always had escorts.

She doesn't seem frightened or concerned.

The voice is almost man-like.

Typically, travel between missions is done in a group and no one sends a nun out to ride alone on the wild and unpredictable prairie.

What's going on with this lone rider?

Something doesn't add up. Don't know what. Just don't like the feel of things.

6

MYSTERY

THE CHUCKWAGON HAS ITS SHELVES AND CUPBOARDS open, flour scattered on the fold-down prep table, and various kitchen utensils hanging from a strap strung across the back of the wagon. Manolito carefully lowers the Dutch oven lid back onto the biscuits. Everything is coming along fine.

Angus leaps up, throwing his plate on the ground and knocking over his cup of coffee onto Isaac.

"By the eternal, Angus, that coffee's hot. What has gotten into you?" Isaac mops at the spilled coffee on his pants.

"What is that?" Angus utters, staring open mouthed as two riders approach the camp.

"Not what, who?" corrects Isaac, standing and looking in the direction Angus points. "Glory be. Who has Chad managed to tow into camp now?"

"It is a nun, no?" says Manolito staring at the riders.

The three men watch as Chad dismounts and ties his horse to the picket line. He wraps the mule's reins over the rope and assists Sister Maria to dismount. They walk to the fire.

"Hell's bells. Oh, pardon me, Sister. What have you gone and done Westerman?" asks Angus.

"I've found our lone rider."

"The one watching us from the hilltop?" asks Isaac.

"The one and same. Let me introduce you men to Sister Maria from San Antonio."

"*Bueno dias*, Sister," says Manolito snatching his sombrero from his head.

Angus nods and touches his hat brim.

"A pleasure," says Isaac.

"Please, don't let me interrupt your meal," says the nun.

"Take a seat over here," Angus says, stepping away from the log lying beside the fire. "It's a better spot to sit."

"Thank you," replies the nun stepping to the space vacated by Angus. "May I have some of that wonderfully smelling coffee?"

"*Si*, Sister. I will get you some." Manolito scrambles to find a clean cup and pours the coffee. He extends it to the nun.

"Manolito, toss me one of those fresh-baked biscuits," says Chad. The cook pitches one still steaming to Chad, who juggles it between his hands.

"Sister, I know you'll like this," says Chad tossing the biscuit to the nun.

The nun quickly places the cup of coffee on the ground, puts both legs together, and prepares to catch the warm bread on her lap.

Taking a bite, she says, "You didn't mislead me, Mister Westerman. This is delicious." To Manolito, she says, "Your biscuits are delightful. Thank you."

"I am glad you like them, Sister," says Manolito with a small grin.

"Are you going to tell us where you found the nun and what she's doing out here?" Angus asks Chad.

"The Sister was back down that trail you found and is traveling to a mission in Indian Territory. Since you're the trail boss, she's your responsibility now. I'm done."

"Whoa, Westerman. I've got beeves to wrangle, not nuns."

"Not so, trail boss. Your job is to take care of anything that comes up during the drive. It's nobody else's responsibility."

"You found the nun. You take care of the nun."

"Can't. I don't work for you. Remember?"

"I can't take care of the Sister, the trail crew, and the herd."

"You signed on to be the trail boss. It comes with a lot of demands. This is just one more."

"Chadbourne, I'll label you a lowlife, slap-headed, scoundrel all the way from San Antonio to Abilene if you don't deal with what you dragged in."

"All right. All right. Don't get your britches in a twist, Angus. I'll figure out what to do with her."

"Gentlemen, I can take care of myself," says Sister Maria. "I've managed to come this far without incident and can continue to do so. However, I would appreciate the hospitality of a good meal and place to sleep."

"Sister, you're more than welcome to stay in my wagon," offers Isaac. "You'll not be disturbed there."

"Thank you. If you'll excuse me then, I'm tired and would like to rest before dinner." The nun rises and follows Isaac to his wagon. He helps her inside and returns to the campfire.

"What do we do now, Chad?" he asks.

"We do nothing. We let the nun sleep. Did you feel there was anything strange about the Sister? The way she handles herself. Did her eyes bother you?"

"Can't say they did," answers Isaac, standing and walking to the chuckwagon.

"Why would she be out here alone?" asks Angus. "I understand her claim to be mission bound, but that just don't add up. Why not come in sooner and not stalk us?"

"There's a lot that doesn't add up, but for now it'll just have to wait. Only the Sister's got the answers, and it seems the nun isn't big on talkin' about it," says Chad.

Cowboys arrive at camp as the second half of the crew gets ready to head into Cleburne.

Chad walks to the chuckwagon to filch a lone biscuit and spots Benjamin riding up to the picket line.

"Looks like you survived today's workload and get to go into town, Benjamin."

"Yes, sir. I'm lookin' forward to the barn dance somethin' fierce." The cowboy dismounts and saunters toward the wagon to collect his warbag. "The other guys said the girls are pretty and the fiddle music is great. Cain't hardly wait to get there."

"Well, pace yourself. You can't dance with every girl at once. So, take it easy on them. Spread yourself around some."

"Oh, I will. Excuse me now, Mr. Chad. I got to get cleaned up and ready for town."

"By the way," says Chad. "Remember, you boys all keep together on your way home. We're tryin' to make sure y'all get back safe, especially since Angus is movin' the herd out tomorrow. You'll do that, right?"

"Will do, and I'll make sure the others understand as well."

"Good. Go get ready to have some fun."

Benjamin hustles to join the other cowboys washing themselves in the river.

The fire crackles and snaps, sending sparks spiraling into the night sky. Manolito finishes serving up the last plate of stew and biscuits to the crew. The first watch of nighthawks circles the herd. The cowboys settle onto their bedrolls around the slowly dying fire. Two boys play cards, one softly plays Buffalo Gals on a harmonica, and one rolls over to sleep.

"Isaac, do you think the nun wants something to eat before the food's gone?" asks Chad.

"Strange. I haven't seen her since I showed her to the wagon."

"Maybe you need to wake her and let her know Manolito is finishin' up the evening meal."

Rising, Isaac walks out of the circle of campfire light toward the wagon. Quickly, he rushes back. "The mule is gone."

"What?"

"Gone. Not there."

"Not tied up? Pulled loose?"

"Yes, and how should I know? It is not there."

"Where's the nun?" Chad is up and running toward Isaac's wagon. "Sister. Sister. Are you in there?"

Yanking back the canvas flap, Chad sees no one in the wagon.

"Isaac, the nun's not here. Get one of the boys to find Angus right now."

"On it, Chad." Isaac rushes to the campfire and rousts a cowboy to ride to the herd in search of Angus.

Manolito throws another stack of cow chips on the fire to burn. The men gather around the campfire. Angus snaps questions at Chad. "What do you mean gone?"

"It's real simple, Angus. The nun is no longer here," replies Chad.

"You brought the nun into camp. She went to his wagon." Angus points at Isaac. "Now, you tell me she's left?"

"That's right." Chad shrugs.

"What's goin' on, Chad?"

"You know, you have a way of gettin' to the heart of the question, Angus. How in the blazes would I know what's going on?"

"You brought her. You should know."

"Well, ain't that just like you to fix on that conclusion."

"Gentlemen, this is certainly not helping us to arrive at an appropriate answer to this dilemma. Obviously, it is too dark to track the run-away Sister," Isaac says hoping to end the finger-pointing. "There is no baggage or material evidence left behind to inspect. So, we are left with a gaping hole in our knowledge and investigation."

"Yeah, what he says," adds Chad. "We'll have to wait until daylight to track her. It'll probably give her ample time and distance to avoid capture or return."

"She seemed set on gettin' to a mission in Indian Territory," says Angus.

"I've been chewin' on that since it was said and can't

rightly recall the location of any mission. I may be wrong. The Territory is mighty big, but not one comes easily to mind," says Chad. "We've been up the trail, Angus. You tell me where you've seen the Padres."

"Now that you mention it, I can't say that I've ever seen one north of the Red River. So, maybe the nun is lying?"

"Didn't say that, just said I don't know of any mission. Besides, why lie to drovers intent on helping her? It just doesn't add up." Chad shoves his hat back on his head. "Anything missing from your wagon, Isaac?"

"It appears that three, maybe four bottles of my elixir have been pilfered."

"You mean stole?" asks Angus.

"Yes, absconded."

"You know, Chad, sometimes he's just too hard to listen to. He don't speak plain English. How do you put up with him?" Angus walks toward the campfire.

"Isaac, you could have simply said, 'Yes, stolen.'" Chad shakes his head.

"The fluidity and magnanimity of the English language does not tend to relegation of single monosyllabic responses."

"Stop it. Just stop it, or I swear I'll smash your last cases of snake oil."

"Dear God, don't do that," says Isaac with panic rising in his voice.

"All right, let's focus on dealin' with the problem at hand and quit proddin' Angus. Agreed?"

"Agreed. Morning comes, we begin our search?"

"Now, go make peace or something like that with Angus, okay?"

"Certainly." Isaac walks towards the campfire, stops, looks

back, and says, "Of course I could agree that I am in complete and total compliance with his leadership acuity and authority, or I can simply stick with an apology, if that is appropriate."

Chad throws both of his arms into the air, shakes his head, and waves Isaac toward the campfire. "Go, get it done, Isaac."

Riding down the main street of Cleburne is a bit unnerving for the cowboys. Every business is closed, and nobody is on the street. At the end of town, lanterns suspended from posts surrounding the corral outside of a large red barn shine brightly. Saddled horses are tied to the corral and others mill around inside the enclosure. The barn is a large two-story structure. Low, single story buildings on each side of the tall center section increase its size. The tall double front doors are flung wide open. Light and music spill into the night, inviting everyone close by to stop and investigate the festivities.

Benjamin and the other drovers ride to the corral, dismount, and tie their horses beside others tethered there. One of the sixteen-year-olds, Bucky Adams, stands beside Benjamin. He buffs his boots on the back of his pant's leg and brushes dust from his blue plaid shirt. Adjusting his bandana, he settles his hat on his head.

"Sure sounds like a fine dance, don't it, Benny?"

"That is does, Bucky. How many girls you figure are in there to dance with?"

"One's enough for me."

"The other boys are already headin' inside. We better hurry or the pickin' will be real slim, real fast."

The two boys catch up with their fellow drovers entering

the barn.

Just inside the door sits Cleburne's sheriff leaning back in a straight cane bottom chair. Standing, he confronts the drovers.

"Whoa, boys. Stop right here. Unstrap your hardware and place it on the table. It'll be here when you leave the dance. You'll have no need of it tonight."

Bucky steps up to the sheriff. "Nobody takes my gun. It goes where I go."

"Well, cowboy, we have a problem then. You see, you'll leave that weapon here or my four deputies will relieve you of the pistol." He gestures to four men standing beside him. "Of course, you could leave."

"Bucky, don't be a damned fool over a gun. Put it on the table. It ain't like it's gonna crawl away or somethin'. Besides, it gets in the way of dancin' anyway." Benjamin shoves Bucky forward.

The other cowboys have already shed their weapons and stepped into the barn. Bucky slowly unbuckles his holster, rolls the rig around his gun, and drops it on the table.

"It better be there when I get back, sheriff." Bucky glares at the lawman.

"Don't worry a bit about it, son. It'll be waitin' right here for you." Taking his seat again and leaning back, he waves Benjamin and Bucky into the barn past the deputies.

Benjamin is amazed by the barn washed in light. Lanterns hang high and low chasing any shadows from the main open area. He sees the space crowded with people – young, old, and in between. All are talking, laughing, and dancing. Everything from buckskin shirts to brocade dresses are visible. Benjamin soaks in all the sights and sounds. He turns to Bucky.

"Do you see any girls?"

"Sure do. There's four standin' over by the fiddle player. They're talkin', pointin', and laughin' at us."

Benjamin looks toward the spot where Bucky nods. There are two guitar players, a fiddler, and a man with a harmonica creating music. "That fiddler is sure sawing a fine 'Camptown Races', ain't he?" says Benjamin.

Bucky reaches over and grabs Benjamin's lower jaw. He turns his head toward the girls. "There. That's what's important, you numbskull. The girls, not the fiddler."

Slapping Bucky's hand away, Benjamin replies, "I know that. Just sayin' I like the music is all, and I ain't no numbskull."

"Let's go make their acquaintance." Bucky weaves his way through the crowd toward the young women. Benjamin follows, feeling nervous and uncertain of how to begin a conversation with a young lady. He looks around him and sees some of his fellow drovers bellied up to the food table, some dancing, and others talking with town folks. It appears to him everyone is having a great time.

Not paying attention to where he's walking, Benjamin turns around a split second before colliding with another cowboy. The collision knocks the boy to the floor. He looks to the be about Benjamin's age and dressed the same way with jeans, boots, and a plaid shirt.

He leaps up from the floor and stands toe-to-toe, eyeball to eyeball with Benjamin.

"You just stupid or don't pay no nevermind about where you're walkin', cowboy?"

"I'm sorry, friend. I wasn't payin' attention and didn't mean any harm."

"Sorry, don't cut it. I've a mind to beat the daylights out of a stumblebum like you. Let's take it outside."

"I came to dance, not fight," replies Benjamin. "I'll oblige you, but don't really want to."

"You're chicken, too yellow to fight?"

"Not yellow, not backin' down. Just statin' my druthers."

Suddenly, a young brunette lady shoves herself between the two cowboys. She turns and glares at the boy picking the fight.

"Rusty Barnett, you got no call to cause trouble. I saw the whole thing, and it was an honest accident. Back off and go back to tellin' tales with your buddies. This fellar asked me to dance, and that's what we are fixin' to do. Go on, get along. You ain't fightin' here tonight."

The girl is the same height as Benjamin. She stands with her hands on her hips, her jaw jutted forward, and stares down Barnett. Her hair hangs to her shoulders, and she wears a light green gingham dress.

"April Mason, you're stickin' your nose into somethin' that don't concern you none. Back off." Rusty glares at her.

"We're goin' to dance. You go on. Git. Shoo." April waves Rusty away. She turns, grabs Benjamin's arm, and leads him to the dance area. "You do know how to dance, don't you, cowboy?" She expects him to take the lead.

Quickly recovering his senses, Benjamin reaches out, embraces April, and begins dancing with her.

"What just happened?" he asks.

"Oh, that Rusty Barnett is always lookin' for any excuse to cause trouble. Your stumblin' into him gave him all the reason he needed to ruin a perfectly good party. Are you really a stumblebum?"

Feeling his face flush red, Benjamin replies, "No, ma'am. I ain't no stumblebum. I was too interested in everything going on and not paying attention."

"Do you do that driving cattle?"

Beginning to feel defensive, Benjamin snaps back, "I'm a good drover. One of Mr. Angus' best. I got no reason to explain myself to you."

"You're right. By the way, who are you?"

The music stops, and people begin moving to the food table or into small groups leaving Benjamin and April in the middle of the dance floor.

"I'm Benjamin Johns from Fredericksburg. We're driving cattle to Abilene for Mr. Angus Tremain."

"Well, Mr. Johns, I'm April Mason, born and raised right here in Clebourne."

"Why did you get in the middle of the fracas?"

"I don't like Rusty, and you're cute."

Benjamin knows his face is scarlet. *This girl thinks I'm cute. How do I deal with this? What do I say? Do I agree? I need help.*

Bucky rushes up.

"Y'all look mighty fine out here dancin'. I didn't know you could move your feet like that Benny."

"Who is he?" April nods toward Bucky.

"He's my saddle partner, Bucky Wilson. He's from Fredericksburg, too."

"Mr. Wilson, why don't you go off and find my friends to visit with, Mr. Johns and I are gettin' along just fine." She smiles at Bucky.

"Yes, ma'am. I'll leave you two alone." He quickly walks back to the group of girls standing by the musicians.

The music starts again, and April motions for Benjamin to step to the music. They dance around the room.

"That's my Pa over there watchin' us." April nods toward a tall, big boned man leaning against a barn support post. He wears a buckskin jacket and Levis. His eyes track every step they make. "If he likes what he sees in how you're treatin' me, he'll stay right there. If he doesn't, he'll be out here in a split second, makin' short work of you."

"I'm hopin' he stays put." Benjamin keeps sneaking peeks at the big man as they move around the dance floor.

"I came to dance, Benjamin. Let's focus on that and not my Pa. Where did you learn to dance this well?"

"My Ma. She taught me to dance and told me that every gentleman needed to know how."

"Your Ma is one smart lady. She raised a handsome, mannered, talented son."

Benjamin is swamped. *I know my face is beet-red, and from the smile on April's face, she appears to be enjoying my discomfort. It's time to even the score.* "Why does a girl as beautiful as you stay in Cleburne?"

"Mr. Johns, you are the presumptuous gentleman, aren't you?"

"I only say what I see, Miss Mason. You are quite comely, and I am enjoying your company immensely."

"Are you flirting with me, Mr. Johns?"

"Yes, Miss Mason, just as hard as I can."

Tossing her head back, April laughs aloud, and they continue to swirl around the floor.

The band is gone, the last wagonloads of farm and ranch families disappear, the lanterns are extinguished, the barn is closed up, and Benjamin's said his goodbye to April.

He and Bucky Wilson are the last two cowboys to leave the

barn dance. During the evening, they shared a bottle of Ol' Granddad, purchased from a local cowboy behind the barn. They've steadily drained the contents during the dance, taking short breaks to step outside and draw deeply from the bottle. It tasted better and better to the sixteen-year-olds as the night wore on. The other members of their crew ride in front of them. The two boys mount their horses and slowly follow their departing comrades.

"Come on, Bucky, the others are leavin' us. Get a move on."

"I don't' know how many girls I danced with tonight. I can't hardly feel my feet no more, Benny. Clawin' my way onto this saddle is makin' my stomach turn flips."

"Don't go cry baby on me now. We got cattle to punch after sunup."

"I done believe I been the one that's been punched."

"Come on, spur up, and keep pace with me, we got to catch up to the rest of the crew."

"You go on, I'm makin' my way nice and easy."

"There'll be hell-to-pay tomorrow if you don't roust out to help move the herd. Old Iron Ass Angus will be all over you like stink on cow flop."

"Quit talkin' about that stuff, I'm gonna throw up." He leans over and explosively vomits, spilling the contents of his stomach on a patch of prickly pear cactus.

"You're wasting perfectly good ham, potato salad, creamed corn, and whiskey, you light weight," chides Benjamin.

"Stop it. Make it stop." Bucky whispers as he heaves over and over until there's nothing left. He leans forward onto his horse's neck, groaning in misery as his horse rocks him back and forth.

Benjamin spurs his mount to close the gap between the crew and himself.

"You trail along back there groanin' and all. I'll check on you in a bit."

"You know where to find me," croaks Bucky as he wipes his vomit specked mouth on his shirtsleeve.

"Help. Help. Help," shouts Benjamin racing into the quiet, sleeping camp. Cowboys spring from their bedrolls. Angus is up and waving for the rider to shut up.

"You damned fool, stop screaming. You'll spook the cattle." He grabs at Benjamin's horse's bridle.

Chad is up running toward the ruckus.

"What's the problem? What's goin' on? Who's hurt?"

"I done like you said, Mister Chad. Bucky was sick and followin' behind. He was there one minute and gone the next. I swear, we rode back together, but now he's not there." Benjamin jabbers while tears stream down his cheeks.

Angus looks at the rest of the crew who arrived shortly before Benjamin came rushing into camp. "Y'all see anything? Did you see where Bucky went? Speak up. Anybody?"

The oldest rider says, "Mister Angus, we didn't see nothin'. Benny and Bucky was laggin' behind, no more than a quarter of a mile. Benny caught up with us, and after ridin' with us for a couple of miles, he went back to check on Bucky. We came on to camp. Next we saw was him charging in here."

"Give me four riders, now, to go help the night hawks settle the herd. Four more of you mount up and ride back with Benny to check the trail. I want Bucky found and found now. Am I clear?" Angus stands with his hand on his hips giving orders.

The cowboys nod, saddle their picketed mounts, and gather

together as they ride into the darkness.

"'Bout how long to dawn, Manolito?" asks Chad.

"No more than two hours, *señor*. The last night hawk watch wakes me up when they leaves camp. *Señor* Russell, he already leaves to bring in remuda when Benny rides into camp."

"Isaac, get a horse from the remuda. Have Russell help you get it saddled and ride out to meet us. Angus let's ride." Chad saddles, mounts, and spurs his horse after the cowboys back-tracking their trail to camp. Angus' horse gallops up beside him.

"You thinkin' what I'm thinkin'?"

"I'm thinking we might be a smidge too late," whispers Chad.

"Even got a good guess where Bucky might be?"

"Somewhere out in the open, easily seen, and it ain't gonna be pretty."

"You know why?"

"No clue."

"You know who?"

"No clue."

"Ain't much at detecting, are you?"

"You might say downright pathetic."

"I'm takin' two boys to the north. You take the other two along with Benjamin to the south. See anything, fire two shots. I'll do the same."

"Shouldn't you stay with the herd?"

"I'm damned tired of writin' letters. Shouldn't you have this mystery solved by now?"

"I'm damned tired of bein' stalked by a maniac." *I'll kill the sonofabitch in an instant when he's found.*

Angus motions two cowboys to follow him and sweeps north.

Chad leads Benjamin and the others as he turns south.

7

RIVER

MORNING FLOODS THE PRAIRIE AS IT ILLUMINATES the riders galloping along the road to town. Chad calls Benjamin over to him. "Where exactly did you leave Bucky?"

"It was over there a piece, Mister Chad." He pulls his horse's reins and lopes a quarter of a mile to the east, circles around staring at the ground, and then spurs his horse into a gallop heading south. Chad and the other two cowboys intercept and stop him.

"There are two sets of tracks heading this way. You see them there?" Benjamin points to the clear prints of two shod horses moving fast. The hoof prints dig into the prairie sod and cast dirt behind them.

"You've found them. Now, let's do this together," says Chad.

He motions for everyone to keep up as he sets out following the tracks. They ride quietly and quickly over rolling hills, through wooded thickets, and back onto open prairie. In the distance, a thin wisp of barely visible smoke smudges the morning air.

Chad motions for the two cowboys to hang back. Calling Benjamin to follow him, he spurs his horse into a gallop, charges up and over the next hill, and in the distance sees a smoldering fire. A ground-tied horse stands quietly beside a fire pit of dying coals. A spit, similar to one used to roast beef halves, is set up. Tied with wire to the horizontal rod is an un-distinguishable charred body. It is hanging face down over the pit where flames once leapt. Chad pulls his rifle, slows his horse to a walk, and carefully scans the open prairie lit by dawn's soft light. There is no sign of movement.

Charging past Chad, Benjamin screams, "Bucky, Bucky." Racing up to the grotesque figure, he slides from the saddle of his still moving horse, lifts one end of the spit off the frame, and slides the body to the ground. Tears stream down his face. Greasy soot covers his clothes and boots. The air reeks of burnt flesh. Clutching the charred remains, he sits in the ashes, and rocks the body of Bucky back and forth.

"Why, Mister Chad? Why?" His tear-stained, ash-covered face begs for answers.

"I don't know, Benjamin. I just don't know. He's gone now. You have to let go so we can bury him. The other boys are coming over the hill. Get up and pull yourself together."

Chad points his Winchester skyward, fires one shot, levers, fires again, and slides the rifle into its scabbard. He dismounts and walks slowly around the fire, pulls his notebook from his pocket, and reads his notes. Taking out his stubby pencil, he quickly jots down his observations. He notes what is evident at the scene, and he considers what is not obvious. There may be a way to make a connection with what is omitted. He closes the notebook and sticks it back into his pocket.

With tears running down his face, Benjamin pulls Bucky's slicker from behind his saddle, lays it out on the ground, and rolls it around the corpse, pulling it closed over the body as the other two cowboys ride up.

"Both of you head back to the hilltop and wave Angus and the others over to us when you spot them. They'll be comin' on the run. Keep a sharp lookout. You watch us, and we'll watch you. Got it?" says Chad.

"Yes, sir." Neither boy asks to see the grizzled remains under the slicker. They appear to accept Benjamin's tear-stained, greasy, sooty, ash-covered appearance as enough for them. Turning their horses away, they lope up the hill to stand watch.

"I only left him for a few minutes, Mister Chad, only a few minutes. I heard him behind me. Nothin' alarmed me. I didn't desert him. You told us to take care of each other, and I did." Benjamin sits hunched over on the ground beside his friend.

"I believe you, son. I don't think you ever wanted this to happen. I do need you to think hard about the ride. You clear headed enough to do that?"

"I think so. What are you askin'?"

"What did you see, or better yet, what didn't you see around y'all when you went forward to catch up with the crew?"

"That's just it. Nothin'. It was black all around. Stars was twinklin', but it was pitch black otherwise."

"No reflections? No sudden flashes of light? Was there any motion or movements out of the ordinary? Anything?"

"Bucky was sick, heavin' up everything he had. I know I heard the sound of horses walkin'. They were ours, or the crew in front. The sound might have been behind us. I don't know."

"How long did you leave Bucky alone?"

"It couldn't have been ten minutes. I galloped up to the crew, about a quarter mile. Told them we were followin' and trotted back to where I left Bucky. He'd disappeared. I looked all around, galloped back down the trail about a mile, turned around, and raced to camp. That's all I know."

"All right. Get him trussed up in your slicker so we can take the body back to camp." Chad notices the two boys on the hill waving their hats.

Angus and the other riders are coming fast.

Chad watches sunrise sweep across the prairie.

Where are you, you evil sonofabitch? Where are you? I'll find you and you'll pay for what you've done.

From a nearby hilltop, ebony eyes pull back from carefully shaded binoculars. A sinister smile spreads across the face as a shadow moves away from the crest of the hill.

Chad rocks along with the motion of his horse. They are traveling just ahead of the drive. Isaac's wagon rattles along beside him. The herd is in motion and slowly moving north.

"Sure was quiet when we buried the Wilson boy," says Isaac.

"Yep. I think everybody is feelin' the pain," replies Chad.

"Did you keep an eye on Benjamin?"

"I was watchin' the boy in particular."

"His anguish over what has transpired is intense. He did not appear to be able to stop crying."

"He's blamin' himself. Don't do no good, but it's hard to break that feelin' once it settles on you."

"Sounds like you speak from experience."

"All of us have somethin' that we carry guilt about. We learn to live with it and go on, or it swallows us whole. He's got good instincts and will probably throw the rope of grief, but it may take a spell."

"I haven't heard anybody talk about the nun. Wonder what happened to her?"

"I forgot about her with all the action around Bucky's death."

"Should we try to locate the sister and protect her?" Isaac glances around the landscape as if looking for the nun. "Do we just forget about her?"

"I'm concerned about her, that's for certain, but with Bucky's burial and Angus' damned determination to move the herd, the sister's disappearance got left in the dust." Chad takes off his hat and wipes his brow with the sleeve of his shirt. He places his hat back on his head.

"Do you see any coincidence between her vanishing and Bucky?"

"What's your point, Isaac?"

"It's just this. The nun leaves. The boy dies. I wonder if there's a connection?"

"Do you believe there's a link between the nun and Bucky?"

"I don't know, but when you were on the prairie, did you see anybody else out there?" asks Isaac.

"I didn't see anybody, and Angus' bunch didn't either."

"So, what happened to the nun?"

"After everybody rode out and back, scoured the

countryside, and moved the cattle, we lost any chance of find-
ing the nun's trail. There were so many tracks that trying to dis-
tinguish those of a mule in all that mess would be impossible."

"That's why you did not stay?" asks Isaac.

"I'm all about detecting but need to do it before everything
is stirred up."

"If Angus had not been so determined to move the herd, we
might have been able to pick up tracks."

"He was hell-bent on moving, even at midday, to put space
between Bucky's grave, Cleburne, and the herd. He's goin'
to drive into the evening to make as many miles as he can.
Somehow, I think it's cleansing for him. At least it's something
he can control and accomplish. Saving one of his cowboys was
beyond his control. It ain't easy bein' trail boss." Chad stands in
his stirrups and looks back at the advancing cattle herd.

"It is not easy on any of us. We all deal with it in our own
way. I cannot stop thinking about the nun. Is she a victim, too?
Why did we not find her body? What if the Sister has something to do with Bucky's death? I know it is almost sacrilegious,
but what if things are not what they seem? What are your
thoughts?"

"Isaac, you're one devious thinkin' cuss." Chad settles back
onto his saddle. "There's something about that nun doesn't fit.
Your questioning clears it up for me."

"Okay. What?"

"When you were a sprout watching your mom shell beans
or slice apples, and someone tossed somethin' for her to catch,
what'd she do?"

"She caught it, of course. I am missing your point."

"My point is - how did she catch it?"

"She sat there, let the item drop into her skirt, picked it up, and dealt with whatever was tossed. Wait. Wait, just a minute." Isaac's expression is one of sudden understanding. "I believe I am getting your point."

"How do you catch stuff in your lap, Isaac?"

"Oh, hell. How could I have been so blind? I always catch stuff on my legs. My mother used her skirt to catch items. The sister used her legs together to catch the biscuit. So, you are saying the nun is…a man?" Isaac sits back in sudden awareness.

"I'm sayin' a lot of stuff don't add up. The dark staring eyes, the low voice, and catching in the lap are all…wait, a lawyer friend taught me this word, *circumstantial*. It means by themselves they ain't enough to prove anything, but it sure does cause one to wonder. Besides, no padre would let a nun travel this country alone."

"Why would a man dress up like a nun and stalk a trail drive? That doesn't make any sense." Isaac shakes his head as if in disbelief.

"Why would someone kill innocent cowboys in the manner they're killed? Most the time crazy don't make sense."

"Yes, but crazy like a fox. Who would be alarmed or frightened if a nun rides up to them? Better still, who would not go out of their way to help a Sister?"

"Now you're startin' to see the picture from my saddle, Isaac. Hey, the disguise worked on me, and I'm the master detective." Chad lets loose a self-deprecating chuckle. *Some detective I am. Cowboys dying all around me, and I can't figure out who's doin' the deed. Maybe, I just need to stick with punchin' cows instead of tryin' to use my head.*

"What do we do now?" asks Isaac. "Do you think the nun will keep on being a nun?"

"Don't know," replies Chad.

"Is she on the run? Where is she now?"

"Can be anywhere."

"Will she continue to victimize this drive?" Isaac seems to become more agitated with each question.

"Lordy, Isaac, you're full of more questions than I've got answers for right now. Not bein' crazy, and kindly don't respond to that statement, I don't begin to know what the nun will do. I don't think we'll see the Sister again until she or he wants to be seen. This means it's even more important to watch our back trail."

"What about the trail drive?"

"The message is loud and clear to Angus and the boys. Watchin' each other's back from this point on will make them harder targets. I believe the Sister will find other victims for the time being. Of course, what do I know? I'm the jasper that brought the fox into the hen house."

"Don't beat yourself up, Chad. You had no idea."

"Yeah, but Bucky weighs heavy on me. I feel for Benjamin. We've a lot in common."

"Heads up, Chad. Russell is driving the remuda past us. It appears that Angus is turning the herd onto bedding grounds for the night. Didn't realize it's almost sundown. We need to catch up to Manolito. You lead out, I'll follow."

The herd has stopped and is milling around as it settles down. In the distance a steady lowing and mooing is heard. A continuous moaning and lamenting of bunched together cattle increases in intensity and becomes a continuing cry. Chad pulls up his horse beside Isaac's wagon as he listens.

"I thought we'd never get here," says Isaac, taking his hat off and wiping his brow. "We are close to Red River Station, are we not?"

"We ain't there yet. You hear that bellerin'? Don't think we're gonna get much closer. Angus has stopped the herd. He's headin' this way." Chad pushes his hat back on his head and settles into his saddle. "He appears to be…what's your word for it? Oh yes, perplexed."

"Do not be condescending, Chadbourne, it does not become you." Isaac glares at Chad.

Angus stops his horse's lope and walks toward Isaac's wagon. "You hear 'em, don't you?"

"I do," responds Chad.

"What're you figgerin'?"

"Don't."

"What'd you mean 'don't'? You've been up this trail as much as me. You know what that noise means."

"You best find a soft spot to settle. The Red River is not cooperatin'."

"I'm takin' my top hand and goin' to see what's between us and the crossing. You stand by in case something comes up?"

"Don't work for you."

"Galldarnit, Chadbourne. I'm askin'."

"Since you're askin', I'll oblige. While you see how many herds are between the river and us, I'll babysit your longhorns and the boys."

"We'll be ridin' into Red River Station as well, could be back late."

"We'll get by. Drink a beer for me at the saloon."

"Dadburnit, Chadbourne. I ain't stoppin' in no saloon," Angus fires back, his face turning a slight shade of pink.

"If it was me, I'd stop at the saloon."

"Well, I ain't you, and I thank God daily for that." Angus yanks his horse around, waves for Benjamin to join him, and weaves his way through cattle toward Red River Station.

"Why do you antagonize Angus in that manner?" asks Isaac.

"If you're askin' 'why do I mess with him', the answer's because it's good for him," replies Chad.

"How can your verbal jousting possibly be beneficial in this regard?" Isaac asks with a lift of his chin.

"Damned if Angus ain't right. Can you just speak plain English? I spend half my time deciphering what you're sayin'."

"Don't you start with me," Isaac chides, "I'm the only one really on your side. However, not necessarily by choice, more by threat."

"Whatever it takes." Chad grins at the snake-oil peddler. "We're together through this whole shebang."

"So. Again, I ask you, why antagonize Angus?"

"I've known Angus for a long time. Our backgrounds are a whole lot alike. He always comes up with the right answers. I just keep 'his pot stirred' until he gets there. Kinda simple really. Besides, he'd think somethin' was wrong if I didn't. You understand?"

"No. Probably never will. Are we going to Red River Station? After two weeks getting here, I would like to view the town."

"We'll go soon. The river is flooding from upstream and has to let off steam on this end. We'll be here for three or four days before some trail boss will brave the crossing. If his cattle and him drown, we'll wait longer. If he gets across, 'Katie bar the door,' they'll start puttin' cattle across in a steady stream."

"Why do we all have to cross here?"

"We don't have to, but buffaloes and Indians have been using it since forever. Spanish Fort is downstream, and the ford is fair. When herds stack up here, others go there. Colbert is a little further and has more quicksand, but the river can still be forded. There's a ferry as well. Here is the best place to cross because the bend in the river throws the current hard against the south side. This creates sandbars allowin' cattle to walk across the better part of the river before swimmin' a narrow channel."

"When the Red River floods, I guess that disappears?"

"When the river floods, it runs bank-to-bank, deep as a well, draggin' heavy brush, broken trees, and stumps plucked out by their roots swirlin' and bobbing downriver. I believe the river upstream is scoured clean all the way to the *Llano Estacado*."

"The 'yanno' what?"

"The *Llano Estacado*, the 'staked plains,' West Texas plains. Treeless rolling grasslands go on for miles and miles. The pioneers used to drive stakes in the ground to find their way out and back. So, 'staked plains' or as the Mex say, *Llano Estacado,* became its name."

"Mister Westerman, you're just full of interesting facts, aren't you?"

Chadborne doesn't miss Isaac's sarcasm or the rolling of his eyes. "I try to please, Isaac. Yes, indeed, I try to please. I need to go check on the cowboys. Why don't you head over to camp and help Manolito and Russell? I'll join you later."

Chad rides toward the herd as Isaac steers his wagon toward the campsite.

The campfire flames leap into the night sky. Cowboys sit on their opened bedrolls some distance away from the flames. Angus stands close by the firepit. "We're about five miles from the river and have four other herds in front of us," he says. "The river is dropping. Been going down for a few days. We'll have to sit tight for maybe another three or four days before giving it a go to cross."

"Our boys goin' to help the others over?" asks Chad.

"Yep, we'll pitch in with a few boys to help. Most of our crew will hold our herd, but three or four can help the other outfits. We'll get help in return when it's our turn. Seems like the right thing to do."

"That it does." Chad tosses coffee grounds from his cup into the fire. "Since you're back, I'm gonna take Isaac into town tomorrow. Do you want Manolito to go in and replenish his chuckwagon? This is last real stop before Kansas to get that done."

"If you'd have waited a minute, Chad, I was fixin' to ask you,"

"Sorry, Angus. Just jumped the gun on you."

Angus turns toward the chuckwagon. "Manolito, can you be ready to go to town with Chad and Isaac tomorrow?"

"*Si, Señor* Angus. I will pick up frijoles, coffee, flour, salt, and sugars. It should be enough."

"Peaches." Chad announces. "Don't forget canned peaches, Manolito."

"*Ah, si, si. El Durazno*, peaches. They are *bueno* in the cobblers, no?" A smile spreads across Manolito's face.

"Your cobbler creations are masterpieces of epicurean delight and delicacy, Manolito," says Isaac.

"If that is good, *Señor* Isaac, then *bueno*. Sometimes I know not what you talk about."

"Don't worry, Manolito." Angus sighs as he pours another cup of coffee.

"We don't understand him either."

8

RED RIVER STATION

THE CATTLE BLANKET THE LANDSCAPE COVERING hills and valleys. Isaac rides beside Chad wending their way through the herds waiting to cross the Red River.

"There is nothing but miles and miles of cattle. There must be ten thousand bovines between us and the river." Isaac strains his neck looking around at the longhorns.

"Yes. Angus says we have four herds in front of ours. Looks like they're spread all over tryin' to graze on whatever they find. The cowboys try keepin' the herds apart, but sometimes it's impossible. Sorting out brands is the devil's work to do."

"What about those herds behind us. What graze will be left for them?"

"That's their worry. Their trail bosses will have to figure out what to do when they get here." Chad shrugs his shoulders.

"What about my wagon?" Isaac suddenly asks.

"Relax. Russell has a wrangler driving it. Everything is all right."

"All my pharmaceuticals are in it. My livelihood. My elixirs."

"Your snake-oil."

Isaac stands in his stirrups looking forward. His foot slips, and he struggles to catch himself before falling from his horse. "Is that Red River Station?"

Chad nods. "Yes. We're headin' toward those twelve lumber-built buildings up there."

"The town looks small for all I have heard about it."

"The Station's important as an outfitting post for trail drives."

"That seems to be evident with all the cattle amassed here."

"The trail to the crossin' runs between the town and Salt Creek that flows into the Red River. The Post Office is called Salt Creek, but every drover knows this spot as RedRiver Station."

"The Federal Government calls it one name, and the drovers call it another? I do not understand." Isaac squirms in his saddle attempting to find a soft place to sit.

"I guess the *station* moniker kind of stuck from Confederate army days and the old stockade that sits outside of town on the river's bluff," Chad explains.

"How do folks stand the dust and smell from all these cattle?" Isaac wrinkles his nose and sneezes.

"It's good for them. All these folks call that smell business."

"Okay. Whatever you call this place, it is finally good to arrive," says Isaac. "I am so parched that my mouth feels like burnt cotton. It is truly incumbent on us to find the nearest tavern and partake of a beverage. I need a beer."

"We need to wash up."

"I would rather have a beer, as pleasant as washing up and being clean again might feel."

"We'll get that after Mollie's."

"What's Mollie's?" Isaac's horse walks down the road leading to town.

"J. S. and Mollie Love built the two-story hotel you see over yonder." Chad points out the building. "She sets the best table in this whole part of Texas. Every cowboy knows Mollie Love, and nobody misses stopping. I ain't about to be the first."

"I will wash up for that," says Isaac.

"Thought you might."

Chad sets an easy trot toward the hotel. Isaac follows.

Isaac and Chad walk into the restaurant freshly washed up with the dust brushed from their clothes. Chad sees eight tables arranged around the room. Two waiters rush between the kitchen's swinging doors and customers seated at the tables. Three floor-to- ceiling windows along the front wall let light spill into the room. Two seats open up at a table, and Chad ushers Isaac over to sit down.

Platters of fried chicken are handed around the table, followed by bowls of mashed potatoes, a glass boat filled milk gravy, and plates covered with biscuits.

Conversation flows around the table as if everyone is trying to talk at once. Chad motions for Isaac to take some and leave some as the dishes and bowls pass by.

Wiping his hands on the cloth napkin, Chad pushes back from the table in the Love's Hotel. Patting his belly, he says, "That's just about the best fried chicken I ever ate."

"I do believe that Manolito's culinary expertise has been surpassed. This meal was sumptuous. The apple pie is divine." Isaac forks the last crumbs from his plate.

A middle-aged woman walks through the swinging kitchen door and into the dining room. Her cotton dress has ruffles at the shoulders, and she wears a full-bibbed apron. She brushes back strands of brunette hair from her face, leaving flour streaks on her flushed, smiling cheeks. Waving at others in the room, she walks over to Chad and Isaac.

"You boys get your fill?"

"Yes, and it was good. Nope, better than always," says Chad. "Mollie, this is Isaac Wisenheimer. A traveling pharmacist." He points at Isaac. "This, my friend, is Mollie Love, a genuinely wonderful lady."

"Pleased to meet you, Mrs. Love." Isaac stands, takes her hand, places it to his lips, and bows from the waist. Looking Mollie in the eyes, he says, "Your culinary talent is beyond comparison. I would say it is phenomenal."

"My, he does act and talk flowery, don't he?" says Mollie with a smile. "I like it. You're always welcome here, Mr. Wisenheimer."

Removing her hand from Isaac's grip, Mollie turns to Chad.

"You'll see that the rest of your crew stops by, won't you?"

"Couldn't stop them if I tried, Mollie. Ol' Angus and Russell will scorch a path gettin' here."

"I got to get back in the kitchen. Got skillets cookin'. Always good seein' you boys." Hiding a smile behind her hand, she says, "Pleasure meeting you, Mr. Wisenheimer." Turning she hurries back toward the kitchen.

"My pleasure, Mrs. Love," Isaac replies. "She is a delightful lady, Chadbourne." He sits.

"One of the best. I've got to stop at the leather store and mercantile. You goin' with me or restin' here for a spell?"

"I suppose I will go with you. Maybe we can stop at the saloon for a drink."

"Sounds like a plan, Mr. Wisenheimer." Chad leaves a gold eagle on the table for the meal.

They stand and quickly move out of the way as two more patrons rush to take their vacated seats. Walking from the hotel, they mount their horses, and ride to the other end of Main Street, reining to a stop in front of Thurston's Mercantile store. Across the street is the saloon.

Chad walks into the leather store and greets the cobbler. "Friend, I hear you make the best boots north of San Antonio. Is that so?"

"I don't know about the best, but I make them the best I know how," answers the thin man rising from the treadle and hand-cranked stitching machine in the back of the store. Tables on both sides of the narrow room are covered with tanned hides and swatches of cloth. Wiping his hands on the bib-front leather apron, he extends his right hand to Chad.

"Good to see you again, Chadbourne. It's been a while."

"Sure has, H. J. Been too long. How's the boot business?"

"I'm making a living at it. Drovers keep coming in and ordering boots. You ready for a new pair?"

"No. This pair I've got on are just gettin' broke in. You

97

made 'em just fine. It's for my partner over here." Chad reaches over and grabs Isaac by the arm, moving him toward the boot maker.

"Wait, wait, just a minute." Isaac yanks his arm away from Chad. "Who said I needed any boots?"

"You can't ride where we are goin' and get along with those store bought shoes of yours."

"These shoes have done me fine so far. I will have you know that…"

"Those round-nosed, high-top, button-over, flat heeled spats aren't going to get the job done where we're headed."

"I suppose only boots will do?" asks Isaac.

"Do you know why we wear boots?"

"I do not have the slightest idea. Why?"

"Because they are built to work with our saddles, and we spend from sunup to sundown on horseback."

"What are you talking about?"

"The boots are pointed to slip into the stirrup quick and easy. The tall heel catches on the stirrup and keeps your foot in place. The tall uppers protect your ankles from stickers and thorns. You beginnin' to understand?"

"All right, I get the picture, but what has that to do with me?"

"You and I are goin' to be doin' some hard riding real soon. You need the equipment to do the job."

"Hard riding? Where, when, how hard?"

"I'll tell you later. Right now, shuck them shoes you're wearing and plant your foot on that piece of scrap leather." Chad hands Isaac a piece of cut up leather.

"H. J., I know you build to order, but might you have a pair or so on hand to fit my friend?"

"Chad, you know I only keep boots on hand for them that ordered a pair."

"What about that line of boots on the shelf along the wall. There must be fifteen or twenty pairs of boots there," says Isaac pointing to the shelf.

"Friend, them boots are for cowboys who ordered a pair of boots made for them on their way to Kansas. I have the boots waitin' for them to come home. Them up there ain't never been claimed. Their owners never made it back to Texas."

"You are going to leave them there? They are perfectly good boots to sell."

"Yep. My shop, my boots, and that's where they'll wait for their owner."

"Do you have a spare pair on hand?" asks Chad.

"I did build some extra pairs a while ago, in my spare time. Step on the leather and let me get a carbon outline of your foot." The boot maker kneels down and traces around Isaac's foot on the scrap leather. "Grab a sit. I'll be right back." He disappears into a back room.

"All those boots up there are for cowboys not coming back to Texas?" asks Isaac looking at the shelf.

"Yep. Those boys tangled with stampedes, Indians, rustlers, got snake bit, or drowned. They ain't comin' home," answers Chad.

"Or, they were killed by a fiend like the one we are tracking," whispers Isaac.

"Maybe that, too."

"You're in luck, friend," says the boot maker walking toward Isaac. "Try this pair on. Sit down, put your foot in, grab the loops at the top, and slide 'em on."

Isaac slides on one boot and the next. He stands and stomps

both feet on the floor.

"They are snug but comfortable." He walks around, appearing to enjoy the black stovepipe boots.

"Need to be snug to start with, they'll fit real nice that way," replies the boot maker.

"What does my friend owe you, H. J.?" Chad indicates for Isaac to pay for the boots.

"Them's nothin' special. How's three dollars sound?" asks the boot maker.

"Pay the man, Isaac. Thanks, H. J. I'll make sure the boys on the crew stop by before we move out."

"Be obliged to you Chad. Let 'em know that H. J. Justin makes fine boots. They'll not be disappointed."

Isaac walks with a pronounced lift of his chest, and a stride that rolls his boots from heel to toe, careful not to scuff his new footwear.

That's some rockin' chair cowboy, thinks Chad as he watches Isaac's proud prance.

Isaac and Chad find a table by the back wall of the cool, dark saloon. The bar runs the length of one side of the room, and the bartender methodically cleans shot glasses stacked beside him. The front windows and batwing doors allow light to filter into the space. The building across the narrow alleyway shades three windows along the side of the saloon. The table beside them is the only other one occupied of the seven scattered around the space. Three drovers sit, talking quietly.

"It was the damnedest thing I ever saw," says one with a drooping mustache.

"Tell me. I wasn't there," says his bucktoothed friend.

"We are heading home, north of the Red apiece, lost most of the herd in the flash flood and stampede, ain't nobody happy at all about goin' home."

"Yeah, yeah, what about what you saw."

"Give him time." The third drover with the sombrero speaks up.

"We're riding over a hill, passin' a grove of Oak trees, and hangin' there, with his hands and feet lashed up between two trees, is this Indian."

"No," says Bucktooth.

"Sure as sin. He's hangin' there split open throat to crotch. Everthin' is just hangin' out. Three feathers from each of his braids just flutterin' in the breeze."

"Can't be. I've never seen nothin' like that." Bucktooth folds his arms sitting back in the chair.

"It's true," says Sombrero. "I seen it too. Never figured somebody could do something like that to another person. It's somethin' that Comanches do, and they do bad shit."

"What did you do?"

"Took him down and buried him. That's what."

"An Indian?"

"Wasn't right to do otherwise. He deserved to be buried."

"Well, I'll be. It must've been bad," says Bucktooth.

"Badder than anything I ever seen," says Mustache.

Chad is listening intently to the drover's conversation.

"Isaac, we've seen that knife work before. You hearin' all this?"

"I hear it, Chad," Isaac says with a slow nod. "I know."

Leaning over, Chad interrupts the huddle of men. "Cowboys. Sorry to overhear your conversation. Sounds like you've seen a sight. We were down around Fredericksburg and come upon somethin' like what you're describing."

"Friend, we ain't by Fredericksburg. What I saw was ten miles north of here in Indian Territory, and my story ain't none of your damned business," says Mustache.

"Again, sorry. Didn't mean nothin'." Chad turns his attention back to Isaac.

The three drovers stand and walk out of the saloon.

"Same fiend?" asks Isaac.

"Sure sounds like it could be."

"What's our next move?"

"We let Angus know, and then we'll ride out before the herd moves to take a look see."

"You me—to Indian Territory?"

"That's the direction we're headin'."

Isaac leans forward. "You do know there are Indians there, right?"

"Bunches of 'em."

"Being with you does have its drawbacks, and this is a big one."

"We ain't gonna live forever, Isaac."

"Living a lot longer is what I have in mind, and you seem to find ways to jeopardize that happening."

"Let's go. Got to find Angus." Chad pushes his chair away from the table, stands, and walks to the doorway.

Isaac slowly follows. He takes a moment to look back at the partially consumed drinks sitting on the table. "All I wanted was one beer," he mutters, hunches his shoulders, and exits the saloon behind Chad.

Angus sits mounted watching his longhorns slowly graze the rolling hills. The midday sun is warm as it beats down on him. The morning has been exhausting and sweat stains his hat and shirt. His trail hands helped other herds cross the Red River and finally his cattle safely made the crossing. Chad sits on his horse beside him.

"It's been four hard days, Chad. I appreciate your pitchin' in and helpin' get the herds across the Red."

"It took everybody to get those other herds movin' so we could make the crossin'." Chad's mounted with his right leg in its stirrup and his left wrapped around the saddle horn as he rolls a cigarette.

"You still figurin' on riding ahead a ways to look things over?"

"Yep. I don't imagine we'll find the killer—been too long, but we'll take a look at the lay of the land. I picked up one of them little books printed by the Kansas Pacific Railway at the mercantile in the Station. It's kinda' like a road map of the trail north, Ol' Jesse Chisholm's wagon road."

"We been up that a time or two already."

"Checkin' to see how accurate them boys in St. Louis are tellin' about our trail. Be interestin' to check things out some."

"Well, while you're out there sightseein' maybe you could keep your eyes peeled for that fiend that is stalkin' us."

"Sure, sure, Angus. If I can find him, Isaac can talk him to death. That's why I'm takin' him along."

"If someone can be talked to death, Wisenheimer is just the man to do it. Have Russell give you spare horses in case you need to cover distance in a hurry."

"Planned to, Angus. Thanks."

"See you in four or five days?"

"Yep. Four or five."

Angus moves toward the herd and the swing riders.

Chad goes to find Isaac and make certain he is ready to travel by horseback.

Miles ahead of the herd, in a deep ravine shielded from view, and surrounded by stunted trees, a lone figure huddles beside a small fire, waiting for coffee to boil.

He's coming. I know he's coming. It won't be long now.

The obsidian eyes glisten as they stare fixated at the horizon.

9

INDIAN TERRITORY

C HAD SITS ON HIS HORSE SURVEYING THE ROLLING hills, wooded creek bottoms with elm, oak, and pines, and grasslands that are belly deep on the horses.

We've put about twenty miles between the herd and us. This is some beautiful country he thinks. Some fine country indeed.

"Have you seen all you need to see?" asks Isaac. "My back-end is aching from all the riding, but my feet feel fine in these new boots."

"Glad you like 'em, Cowboy. We've gone about far enough. Time to find us a place to camp and wait on the herd."

"Do you see that wisp of smoke ahead?"

"Yep. I've been watching it for a spell. Can just barely make it out."

"I only caught a glimpse of it. What do you think it is?"

"Campfire, grass fire, could be anything."

"Are you going to find out about it?"

"What do you mean 'you'? It's more like 'we' are gonna take a look see. So, don't go wanderin' off anywhere."

"Where can I wander out here that you cannot see me?" Isaac asks spreading his arms and looking around.

"You'd be surprised what can hide down in the creek bottoms and over the next hill. That's what's got me concerned about the wispy smoke. May be somethin' we don't really want to find."

"I do not like surprises, especially in Indian country. Maybe we should just wait here?"

"No. Come on, Isaac. Let's go take a look." Chad nudges his horse into a trot heading downhill toward the distant smoke. Isaac bounces along behind on his mount.

The buggy sits careened on its side. Its wheel shattered. Beside it sits a figure in a black hood and cape poking sticks into a small fire. Chad lowers his binoculars and places them back in the saddlebag. He and Isaac sit on a hilltop overlooking the well-worn cattle trail. Beside the trail lies the buggy.

"Somebody's down there."

"No horse?" asks Isaac.

"Looks like one is layin' on the ground."

"Hurt? Dead?"

"No way of knowin' from here. Let's move down there real slow like." Chad pulls his Winchester and lays it across his pommel.

"Are you considering a trap?"

"Might be. It doesn't make sense to be foolish."

"You do suspect trouble, don't you?"

"Why don't you pull your rifle from its scabbard and have it handy. Put about ten to fifteen feet between us as we ride down there."

Isaac moves his horse as directed, pulls his rifle, and slowly follows Chad. Both men nudge their mounts into a walk toward the disabled buggy.

Chad watches the crouched figure closely as they get nearer. The person appears to be holding the horse's head. With an abrupt move, the figure stands, turns around, and faces the riders. The hood falls back revealing long shining red hair. With penetrating ebony eyes, a woman stares at Chad and Isaac.

"Who are you? What do you want? I'm armed." A revolver rises from within the folds of her cape. It points at Isaac.

"Ma'am. We mean no harm. Saw your buggy from the hilltop. Can we help?" asks Chad.

"Put your rifles away. Don't move fast. Take it nice and easy."

"No disrespect, ma'am. Not puttin' my rifle down until that shooter of yours is holstered."

"Chad, she's pointing that pistol at me. I'm returning my firearm to its carrier." Isaac slips his rifle back into the scabbard. "See it's put away. Now, will you lower your weapon?"

"If your friend does the same, we will have a truce."

"Chad. Put your rifle away. I believe this lady is intent and firm in her demand. Please, do not do anything to antagonize her to bring about irreversible consequences, or my demise."

"She's not gonna shoot anybody or anything," says Chad, stepping down from his horse. He moves toward the woman.

"Stay back, I warn you. Stay back or I'll shoot." She raises the pistol to fire as Chad reaches out and snatches it from her grasp.

She drops to the ground and returns to caressing the horse's neck. She whispers as she soothes the animal. "I couldn't save him, couldn't move him, all I can do is let him know he's not alone. He's dying, isn't he?" Tears stream down her face and drip from her chin.

Reaching down, Chad takes her by the arm and helps the lady to her feet.

"Yes, ma'am. The horse is dying."

"I didn't want that, but I couldn't do anything to stop it."

"Yes, ma'am."

"You're not going to hurt me, are you."

"I told you we're here to help, not hurt you."

Isaac dismounts and rushes to the woman. He slips his hand under her arm to steady her. "Nobody is going to hurt you. You are safe with us."

Her face softens in relief, and her body relaxes.

"How'd you know she wasn't going to shoot you?" Isaac asks Chad.

"She has a single action Army Colt and hadn't cocked the hammer back. She could squeeze that trigger all day and nothin's gonna happen. Here hold this." He tosses the pistol to Isaac, who fumbles with the gun and drops it. With a look of chagrin, Isaac stoops and picks up the firearm.

"I'm gonna take care of the horse, you get the lady situated by the fire, and then we need to talk." Chad looks at the horse lying quiet on the ground. A broke buggy shaft spears into the animal's stomach and protrudes through its side. A large pool of blood attracts flies and other insects. Shallow breathing is the only indication that the horse is still alive. Kneeling beside the horse, Chad gently strokes its cheek. Its eyelids flutter. He slowly pulls his Colt, places the barrel behind the animal's ear, and squeezes the trigger. The pistol shot echoes and rolls across the open plains.

The woman involuntarily jerks at the report of the firearm.

Isaac takes her arm and leads the woman to the fire. He brushes the dust off a large rock with his jacket sleeve and motions for her to sit. *She is gorgeous. Her face, eyes, shape, and smile. Everything about her is perfect*

Looking at the dead animal, she lets out a long shuddering sigh. "He was a good horse. I should have taken better care of him."

"Ma'am." Chad squats beside the fire and changes the subject. "What are you doin' out here alone? You are alone, aren't you?"

"I am, and I'm attempting to locate my father. He left six months ago to take our herd of cattle to the railhead. Nobody has heard from him in all that time. I've been the past two months at Mollie's in Red River Station inquiring of every trail boss about my father. I've decided that the best way to find him is to go to the railhead."

"You are aware that's four hundred miles from here?"

"Yes. It didn't sound that far until I got out here. This prairie goes on forever. I decided the best plan was to follow the cattle trail. It is so rough and rutted that the buggy wheel dropped into a hole, snapped the rim, and the spokes broke. The horse's harness pulled loose, the shaft snapped, and speared the horse. I tried to do something, but all I could do was watch him die." She begins sobbing again.

"Bringing a buggy out here is plain foolish, ma'am," says Chad. "Even heavy wagons have a hard way to go. Didn't anybody tell you that at the Station?"

Isaac waves away Chad's questioning. He takes Abigail's hand in his and pats it to comfort her as she continues to cry.

After a few minutes, she squares her shoulders, wipes her eyes, and looks at Chad. "I had an abundance of advice and recommendations from those at Red River Station. None of it was getting me closer to my father. I decided to dispense with suggestions and take matters into my own hands."

"She talks like you, Isaac." Chad sits back and studies the woman. *She is very attractive. Her red hair sparkles in the sunlight, her face lights up when she smiles, and her eyes are full of spunk when she's riled. Isaac's watching her every movement. I think he's smitten.*

"Who are you and where do you reside?" asks Isaac.

"My name is Abigail Wilson and I am a resident of Smith County, Texas. May I inquire your names and domicile?" asks Abigail.

"My pleasure to respond. I am Isaac Wisenheimer, lately of Bastrop, Texas, and currently in an arrangement of indentured servitude to my partner, Chadbourne Westerman."

"Servitude?" She looks at Chad. "How can that be?"

Isaac clears his throat. "My present occupation required some precipitous departures from various villages south of our present location. Mr. Westerman is good enough to remind me that certain parties may, and probably are, very interested in my whereabouts. He would be obliged to divulge my location should I decline to cooperate with him in an ongoing investigation."

"So, you are an investigator?"

"No, I'm a medical professional by trade, Doctor Wisenheimer."

"Oh, a physician?"

"No, a pharmacist."

"So, you are Chadbourne Westerman and Dr. Wisenheimer, investigators?"

"What my friend is attempting to say, ma'am, is that he's helpin' me track a killer, and I'm keepin' him from those who have complaints about the snake-oil he peddles," says Chad.

"Snake-oil? That's disgusting."

"I wholeheartedly agree, my lady. That is why my elixir contains only the highest quality ingredients, measured and mixed to the most exacting specifications, and delivers the absolute best to those who require it the most. Your humble servant, ma'am." Isaac nods to the woman.

"You do seem more refined and cultured than many of those I've come into contact with over the past months." She casts a quick glance at Chad.

"My lady, I've been educated, mentored, and instructed by some of the best pharmacological paragons in the Eastern states. I am outstandingly proud of my education. May I inquire of yours? You seem very articulate and learned yourself."

"Why, thank you, Doctor Wisenheimer. I am a graduate of public school, top of my class, and matriculated from Baylor Female College. I am a licensed teacher."

"I knew it, I knew I was conversing with someone of knowledge and wherewithal. It is a divine pleasure."

"I hate to pop your bubble of enjoyment," Chad interrupts, "But we are in Indian Territory. That pistol shot will be heard by anybody listening and it's gonna be night shortly. This buggy and horse draw attention like flies are drawn to… Well, they draw attention. Let's find ourselves another spot not so out in the open."

111

"Excellent idea, Chad," says Isaac.

"Glad you like it," Chad replies sarcastically. "Now, you two ride double. Follow me and don't get lost."

"I'll grab my valise," says Abigail. Quickly reaching into the buggy, she snatches her case, pauses to look at the dead horse, and stands ready to ride. Isaac mounts and assists her as she climbs on behind him.

Chad is already mounted and riding away in search of a place to camp.

"I'll grab around you, Doctor Wisenheimer, to stay on," says Abigail.

"Please do and hold on tight." Isaac wears a big grin. He nudges his horse into an easy lope to catch up with Chad.

A sheltered draw surrounded on three sides by trees whose limbs hang over a spring fed creek looks like the best stopping spot to Chad. Riding slowly around the glen, he searches for tracks or other signs that would reveal others have camped in the area. Deer tracks are all that he finds.

He signals Isaac to move to the wooded area as he rides through the trees and stops beside a small pond. Stepping down, he kneels, brushes water bugs and algae from the top of the water, and takes a cool drink.

Yes sir, nothin' like a good drink of water. This spot looks like it will do for the time being. Plenty of wood, water, and cover. Hobblin' the horses, they can forage the grasses.

"This looks like a great spot, Chad," says Isaac arriving. He throws his right leg over his horse's neck, slides to the ground, turns, and assists Abigail as she dismounts.

"A very engaging location, Mr. Westerman," she says.

"I hope you are not uncomfortable sleeping on the ground with two strange men around you," says Isaac. "We are hard pressed to maintain propriety in this wilderness."

"I'm not a shrinking violet, Doctor Wisenheimer. My father raised me to be an outdoors person."

"Pull the bedrolls and saddlebags, Isaac," says Chad. "I'll start a small fire. It'll be dark soon enough. Oh, hobble the horses and turn them out to graze. They'll stay close."

"You seem to be very in charge, Mr. Westerman," says Abigail. "Is this your normal modus operandi?"

"My what?"

"She wants to know if you always act this way, Chad," Isaac walks back from turning the horses out to graze. "Yes, he does."

"Were you askin' because you've got trouble with that?"

"Oh, no. I was simply inquiring. I defer to your judgment." Abigail takes a seat on a nearby rock, watching Chad coax a flame from his kindling.

"Let's talk while we're waiting." Chad adds small twigs to the fledgling flame. "I would like to know more about your father and his herd." He turns to face Abigail. "What's the whole story?"

"Ah, ever the investigator," says Abigail. "I've told you most of the story already. My father was the trail boss of twenty-five hundred cattle. He had six cowboys with him. They were from Fort Worth. He only really knew a couple of them."

"Why did he lead an understaffed drive with riders he didn't know?"

"He wanted to get the drive out early and could not find any cowboys in Tyler, Smith County. The two he did know were *vaqueros* from Van Zandt, County."

"Why did he have to get an early herd on the trail?"

"You are continuing to ask the same question, Mr. Westerman."

"I'll keep at it until I get to the truth."

"Very well, I have not been entirely candid with you."

"I guessed that much."

"You know you can become insufferable rather rapidly don't you?"

"Some folks say I'm even hard to like." Chad gives Isaac a quick glance. "How uncandid have you been?"

"The facts are, there were several macabre horrendous murders of cattlemen in Smith County prior to my father's departure. He wanted to get his cattle to market before everyone was scared off."

"Tell me about the killings. Why do you say they were murders?"

"The methods were gruesome and horrible. They were definitely not accidents but carefully planned."

"By who?"

"That's the mysterious part. Nobody knows. The sheriff is perplexed. He mentioned that maybe someone who fought in the war and whose mind is disturbed because of what he saw or experienced."

"They catch whoever it was?"

"No, the string of deaths left Smith County and moved south. I did read in newspapers of mysterious deaths in Crockett, Nolensville, and Bastrop similar to those in Smith County."

"Anybody have any idea why cattlemen are targets?"

"Nothing makes any sense. Nobody knows why and are glad when the killer leaves."

"Not gone by a long shot, Miss Abigail." Chad stokes the growing flames with small branches.

"The killer may be stalking this drive, my lady," whispers Isaac.

Her hand goes quickly to her mouth as Abigail inhales sharply. "Out here…where we are…now?"

Isaac nods slowly.

Chad turns to give attention to his blossoming campfire.

Morning creeps silently into the cozy tree enclosed sheltered grotto. Rays of sunlight snake through the tree limbs and illuminate the leaf-covered ground beside Isaac and Abigail. Chad stands silently pressed tight against an oak tree. His hand holds his Colt revolver.

Another nicker and slight shuffle shifts his attention to an area just outside the surrounding hackberry bushes. He eases into the brush and sees two Indians sitting silently on their ponies, watching the grotto. They are both dressed in leather pants and moccasins, ride their ponies bareback, and guide with hackamores.

No paint and don't look like they're here to cause trouble. Wonder how long they've been here, I only heard the horse nickering ten or fifteen minutes ago. Chad looks past the two mounted warriors, searching for other Indians. He sees none.

Okay, here goes nothing. He slides between the bushes and walks toward the riders.

"Others still sleep," says the Indian with long braids sitting on a Chestnut horse. "You have been watching us."

"I heard your horses. Why are you here?" asks Chad.

"My brother and I," the rider indicates the other Indian on a black horse, "are searching for our friend."

"He's not here."

"We know."

"You speak English well."

"We are *Chahta*. Missionaries teach us. You white men call us Choctaw." He points to the east. "We find dead horse and wagon. Yours?"

"Yep. Wagon crashed and killed the horse."

"We saw."

"May we pass through your land, or can we expect trouble?"

"You are the only one holding a weapon." Unstrung bows and arrows are in quivers hanging around the Indians' backs. "We should ask you the same question."

Chad quickly slides his Colt into its holster. "Perhaps, we can come to some sort of agreement."

"Does the white man have any coffee?"

"I can fix some right quick."

"We will wait," says the rider on the Chestnut horse. Both Indians slip from their horses and sit cross-legged on the ground.

Chad steps back through the brush, approaches Isaac, and shakes him awake.

"What, what, we don't have to ride yet, do we?" asks Isaac, shrugging off Chad's hand.

"No, but we have breakfast company. Choctaw Indians."

Snapping fully awake, Isaac scrambles for his weapons. Chad places a hand on his arm.

"Slow down. They are friendly, at least for now. Get your wits collected, and we'll talk with them. Wake up Abigail but tell her to keep quiet. No screaming or loud noises."

"You're sure they friendly?"

"I'm still wearing my hair, aren't I?"

"All right, all right. I'll wake Abigail."

Isaac reaches over and places his hand across the girl's mouth.

Her eyes immediately snap open with a look of fright.

Isaac leans over and whispers to her.

She nods her head in understanding and he removes his hand from her mouth.

"How many savages," she asks questioningly.

"Chad did not say but they appear to be friendly. That's what he said, and I believe him."

"We're safe?"

"For now. Be quiet. Move slow and easy, nothing sudden."

"I will. I will. Be assured."

"Good, I'm going to help Chad."

"I'll not budge from this spot."

Isaac turns to Chad who is building the fire and is directed to fill the coffee pot from the pond. Chad digs out a package of coffee grounds from his saddlebag. Shortly, the drink is brewing, and its aroma fills the grotto.

Chad rises and motions Isaac to follow. He steps back through the hackberry bushes where the Indians wait.

Isaac stumbles along.

"Coffee smells good," says the Indian with braided hair.

"We'll give it a few minutes to cook and then drink," replies Chad. "How are you called?"

"I am called *Shikoba*. It means *feather*. My brother is *Isi, deer*."

"I am Chad, and my partner is Isaac." He indicates Isaac standing behind him and staring at the seated Indians.

"Your Isaac is a fearful man," says *Shikoba*.

"Well, your visit has him a mite frazzled."

"What mean you frazzled?"

"Sorry. You've surprised him."

"Ah, good. Him not speak much?"

Chad looks at Isaac who remains staring with mouth agape. "That's part of being frazzled," he says with a smile.

"I will remember frazzled. It is a good word."

"Yep. It comes in handy at times. I'm going to get the coffee."

Chad pushes down on Isaac's shoulder, causing him to sit down. He steps through the bushes. In a few minutes he returns, passes out tin cups, and begins pouring strong black brew from the scarred, beat up pot.

The first taste causes bitter expressions on the Indians' faces.

"Need something. Bitter water," says *Shikoba,* holding up his cup.

Abigail steps through the hackberry thicket holding a sack. She takes a seat beside Isaac. "Good morning, Chad. I see that we have visitors, I thought the sugar would sweeten things." She begins pouring the white powder into the Indians' coffee.

Both braves express surprise on their faces as they stare at Abigail's red hair that appears to flame in the early morning sunshine. They mutter to themselves as they gesture toward Abigail.

"Well done," says Chad. "Like my old momma used to say, 'A little sugar never hurts.' It also appears you've got their attention."

"I've always tried to make a grand entrance and good impression."

"Will you two quit chitchatting," says Isaac. "What are we going to do?"

"I imagine we'll be hospitable and listen. You got a better idea?" asks Chad.

"How is being hospitable to savages going to get us anywhere?" Isaac continues to watch every movement of the Indians. "Hopefully, we will keep our hair."

"You do know they understand everything you're sayin', don't you?"

Isaac quickly looks at the Indians.

"Settle down, have some coffee, and learn something," says Chad.

Shikoba reaches over and gently touches Abigail's hair, drawing back his fingers as if burnt. He looks at them closely. In a swift motion, he pulls his knife and lays the blade against a hank of her hair.

As swiftly, Abigail reaches up and grabs his wrist, stopping any motion of the knife.

Ebony eyes lock together as Indian and woman meet each other's gaze.

Abigail slowly reaches with her other hand, gently tugs the knife from *Shikoba's* grip, and trims a lock of hair. She hands the knife and cutting of hair to him.

Speechless, Chad relaxes his grip on his holstered Colt.

Isaac sits dumbfounded.

Shikoba nods and tucks the lock of hair into a small leather bag hanging from his hip. "It is good."

He begins drinking his coffee.

10

CONTINUING

MOUNTED ON HIS BUCKSKIN, CHAD SITS ON THE LOW grass-covered hill watching the trail herd approach from the south. He thumbs through the notebook he carries in his shirt pocket and reads the notations on each page. Humming softly, *We Shall Gather at the River* to himself, he turns to the next page.

Somewhere in all of this is the answer. I've made notes on each killing. There has to be a thread or link somewhere. A good detective would see it.

Isaac rides up the hillside, and Chad pockets his notebook.

"Damn it, Isaac. I am more confused about that woman than a raccoon washing a cube of sugar. We can't drag her all the way to Abilene with us. Angus will have a fit. He'll boot you and me out of the outfit even for bringing the idea up."

"There is no other solution," replies Isaac, seated on his horse beside Chad. "Who will take her back to Red River Station?"

"Not me. I've got to keep moving with the herd if I hope to catch the killer."

"So, you'll turn me loose to take her back?"

"You'd never make it. You'd end up in some Indian town over Missouri way."

"Looks like there is only one answer then. She will ride with me in my wagon and not bother Angus or the drive."

"You just don't get it do you?" Chad shakes his head. "It's having a woman on a drive. She's no ordinary woman; she's a looker, a real looker. The boys will fall all over themselves when this lady shows up."

"She is very attractive." Isaac pauses to enjoy watching Abigail toss rocks into the nearby stream.

"Oh, go over there and collect her from that creek before she falls in or gets lost. We'll go down and face the wrath of Angus. I hope he doesn't shoot you."

"Why would he shoot me?"

"Because he likes me and already doesn't like you. This may be the last straw."

Chad gently kicks his horse into a walk as Isaac turns to retrieve Abigail.

Sparks scatter and explode skyward. Chad watches a fiery brand spin out of the campfire and land beside a lounging cowboy. Jumping up the boy slaps at the embers on his Levis and kicks the stick back into the fire.

"No way. No how. No time," shouts Angus.

Chad and Isaac sit on the log beside the fire watching his tirade.

"No woman is goin' on this drive. I won't have it. I can't have it. It ain't gonna happen." Angus' face shines cherry red. A collection of spittle forms at the side of his mouth.

"Geesh, Boss, you don't need to kick the fire all over me," shouts Benjamin Johns. The young skinny cowboy slaps at the last few embers clinging to his pants.

"Oh, shut up. I'm talkin' to these two jaspers." Angus points at Chad and Isaac.

"Now, Angus, there's no call to get worked into a lather. You're going to bring on apoplexy carrying on like this," says Chad as he pushes his hat back on his head. "The girl is here, there's no way to get her back to Red River Station, and she'll ride in Isaac's wagon."

"You…you…," sputters Angus. "You know…you know… havin' a woman on a drive just ain't right." He waves his arms around his head caught up in the anger and frustration of his ranting.

"Mr. Tremain, if you will entertain my suggestion…" Isaac begins speaking.

Angus spins, slaps his hand to his holster, and glares at Isaac. A fierce twitch flutters under his right eye. "One more word, *just one more word*, snake oil man, and it will be your last." His voice cracks like a whip. Leaning toward Isaac's ear, he whispers, "Shut the hell up."

Chad throws a protective arm across Isaac. "There's no need to be goin' that far. He didn't mean any harm." Standing, he walks to Angus, places his arm around the man's waist, and lays his hand on Angus' pistol. "We all know it ain't to our liking, but it is what it is. Can we agree to just make the best of things and move this bunch of cattle to Kansas?"

Stepping away from Chad, Angus turns, glares at him, a vein throbbing at his temple, and says, "This is your doin' Westerman. I was doin' right well pullin' together a drive, then up you ride. Now, I'm totin' a snake oil peddler and a school marm. They are your responsibility. Do you hear me?"

"I'm standing right here, Angus. I ain't across the pasture. No need to shout. They're my responsibility. I got it. Are we good?"

"We ain't good by a long shot. We ain't happy. We ain't pleasant. And we damn sure can barely stand it. Ah, hell, all we need is a Fredericksburg German brass band and I'll be leading a parade into Abilene. If you drag one of those in, I'll shoot you. By the everlovin', right between your eyes." Angus stomps off toward the chuckwagon.

Benjamin Johns stands in slack-jawed shock at the recent confrontation. "I ain't never seen the Boss get that heated up over anythin' before. Do you reckon he means it?"

"Well, Ben, if you stumble across a German brass band while you are ridin' point for this drive, you make sure you tell me first. I'll need a ten-minute head start." Chad smiles as Benjamin walks away shaking his head.

Isaac stands. "Am I to assume that Miss Abigail remains with the drive?"

"Oh, she'll remain. We have no option, but there are conditions."

"Should we go discuss those with her?"

"Isaac, you are a man of profound understanding. Yes, Abigail needs to know her limits."

"Thank you, Chad, I try to be erudite on all manner

of subjects. However, females do tend to cause me much consternation."

"I'm not real sure what you just said but figure it amounts to the fact that females are confusing. You're right. This one needs to understand that she's confined to your wagon and has to walk a mile around Angus. Let's go talk with her."

The coffee pot continues to boil on the flat stones surrounding the campfire. Its aroma swirls upward and scatters in the night sky. Leroy grabs a handful of sand to scrub the grease from the frying pan and sets it aside to cool.

"You think that herd is two or three days behind us?"

"Yep." Rafe stretches out on his blanket. "We've been riding steady, and they've crossed the Canadian and comin' up on the Red Fork River. I put us about half way across the Territory."

"Ain't seen one injun yet. Don't that seem strange?"

"Just because you ain't seen them, don't mean that they ain't seen us. I imagine they're watching purty close like."

"You think we need to watch our horses and hair closer than we been doing?"

"If they wanted either one, they'd be gone by now. I believe the herd is their attention."

"You think them injuns'll steal the herd 'fore we do?" Raylin lazily sprawls against a log, scratching under his arm and crotch, chasing vermin. He pulls out a sharpening stone from his saddlebag lying beside him and, taking out his bowie knife, he gently strokes the edge across the stone.

"What use do injuns have herding cattle? They'll steal some for food but not the herd. The worst they can do is scatter it."

Rafe looks at Rooster. "Why does your moron brother look like he's perchin' on his saddle?"

Raylin looks across the campfire and sees Rooster squatted beside the saddle and blanket lying on the ground. "He likes to do that. Ain't doin' no harm. Let him be." He continues to sharpen his knife.

"You know he ain't right, don't you? If he starts crowin' again, I'm goin' to knock him silly."

Rising up, Raylin looks at Rafe. "If you lay a hand on him, it'll be the last time you'll use that hand." He tests the edge of his knife with his thumb and points it at Rafe.

"You keep pushin' me, Raylin, and somethin' is bound to happen." Rafe pauses and looks intently into the night. "Shhhhh. Listen."

In the darkness, Rafe, Raylin, and Leroy hear hoofbeats of an approaching animal.

"Hello, the camp. I smell your coffee. Can you spare a cup?" A low-pitched voice pierces through the darkness surrounding the campfire.

Sliding their hands onto their pistols, the outlaws gently slip back away from the fire and into the darkness. Only Rooster remains perched beside his saddle, clucking to himself.

Suddenly, he stands, flaps his folded arms like wings, extends his neck, and crows aloud.

Into the campfire circle of light rides a nun on a mule.

Abigail, Chad, and Isaac sit on boxes pulled from Isaac's wagon.

Chad scratches the ground with a stick. "Angus doesn't cotton to the idea of women on a cattle drive. Your presence causes the cowboys to lose focus on what they are here to do. These young men will be distracted by you, and when that happens, something bad always follows."

"My, I was not aware that by my very being here would cause such an upheaval." Abigail looks at Chad and Isaac.

"Here's the deal. You will ride with Isaac and stay in and around this wagon. Under no condition will you mingle with the cowboys or go to the campfire for meals. Stay here. Isaac will make sure you eat as good as the rest of us."

"See here, Mr. Westerman, this is a free country, and I can go where I please, when I please."

"No, ma'am, a cattle drive ain't free country. There's one boss, and that's Angus Tremain, and his second is the top wrangler, Russell Thomas. What they say goes. It's the law out here."

"What if I refuse your magnanimous gesture of confinement?"

"Well, we'll be cut loose to fend for ourselves. Out here travelin' in a crowd is always better. You've already experienced doing it alone."

Lowering her head, Abigail stares at the ground. "Yes, I have experienced that."

"It won't be bad, Miss Abigail. My company can be quite stimulating," says Isaac.

"Dr. Wisenheimer, that was never the issue. It's just being told what I can and cannot do that discomforts me. I was never good at limitations."

"This is the deal. Can you buck up and go with it?" Chad stands.

"I suppose I have no alternative. Very well, Mr. Westerman, please convey to Mr. Tremain I will abide by his stipulations. I do not like it, but I will comply."

"Good. The herd is already movin' and we need to catch up with Manolito and the chuckwagon."

The nun sits on the mule taking in the motley cowboys around the campfire. Nobody moves.

"Gentlemen, I smelled your coffee. Can you spare a cup?" the nun asks.

Rafe rises and steps toward the nun. "Climb down and we'll pour you a cup. Leroy, take the mule to the picket line."

Stepping from the saddle, the nun walks toward the campfire and sits down cross-legged beside Raylin.

"What in the blazes are you doin' out here?" Raylin asks.

"I'm heading for the mission in Indian territory."

"I didn't know the Papists had any missions out here."

"It's new, and I'm coming to work with the priest. I'm from San Antonio. Where are you men from?"

"We're from all over ma'am," answers Leroy. "Raylin and Rooster are from East Texas. Me, I'm from Waco, and Rafe is from Fort Worth. We're travelin' to Abilene."

"Shut up, Leroy," says Rafe squinting at the nun. "You're runnin' your mouth too much."

"She asked, I was just bein' polite." Leroy sulks.

"It seems mighty strange what with you ridin' alone out here. You're a long way from any help." Rafe stares at the worn brown mule eared boots the nun wears. "You don't dress like a nun neither."

"How should I dress out here? I always wear my habit, and the boots are much better for riding."

"Somethin' don't fit with you, Sister. Can't put my finger on it, but somethin'."

"While you're trying to figure things out, might I have that coffee?"

Leroy grabs the pot, burns his hand, yanks out his shirttail, wraps it around the handle, and pours another cup.

"How did you men meet up?" The nun sips slowly from the tin cup.

"Raylin and Rooster was travelin' towards Fort Worth, and we met in the saloon in Waco," says Leroy. "They was fresh home from the war. They both was in the 12th Mississippi. That's where Rooster lost his mind. Course his name ain't really Rooster. It's Richard."

"I already told you to shut up, Leroy," says Rafe. "No need for all the talk." *She keeps watching us with those dark eyes like she's trying to read into our souls. She stares at Leroy, Raylin, and me, probing and searching for something.*

"I can talk to whoever I want to, Rafe. You ain't no king over me."

"You idjit. You don't know nothin' about this nun, and you're spillin' your guts."

"That's quite all right. I am simply trying to make your acquaintance." The nun stretches and rises. "I think I will try to get some sleep. Do you mind if I place my bedroll beside the fire?"

"Sleep where you want to, Sister. Just stay in sight. Leroy, grab her bedroll from the mule," says Rafe.

Leroy returns with the bedroll, and the nun places it beside the log where Raylin reclines.

Rooster perches beside his saddle and clucks lowly, Rafe rolls up in a blanket, Raylin throws more wood on the fire, and Leroy curls up in his bedroll.

11

TROUBLES

ORNING FRACTURES THE HORIZON WITH GOLD, yellow, and red sunbeams radiating into the crystal blue sky. Rays of sunlight stab into the wooded thickets along the creek bottoms as it sweeps across the grass covered prairie in rolling waves.

Rafe knows something doesn't feel right. Opening a sleep-crusted eye, he looks around the blackened charcoal fire pit.

Raylin's still leaning back against the log snoring, Rooster's perched beside his saddle with his head lolling to one side, and Leroy's curled up in a fetal position clutching his blanket. Where's the nun?

Rafe throws off his blanket and leaps up. He surveys the prairie around them. *Nothin'. Nothin' movin' out there. Where the hell is the nun?*

Grabbing the frying pan, he bangs it down on the stones around the fire pit.

"What the hell?" Raylin snorts himself awake.

"Who, what…" Leroy clings tightly to his blanket.

Rooster stands, sticks his hands in his armpits, and begins flapping his arms like wings. He throws back his head and sees Rafe standing with the frying pan in his hand ready to swing it. He squats back down and quietly clucks.

"Where the hell is the nun," shouts Rafe. *How could she have gotten away without me hearing her or the mule?*

"I ain't got no idea," says Raylin. "I thought you was watchin' her."

"Ain't nobody watched her it appears," mutters Leroy from under his blanket.

"Well, ain't we a fine bunch of how-do-you-do-its?" Rafe throws the frying pan to the ground. "Somebody waltzes in here, pumps information from us, and leaves without a sound."

"She didn't pump no information." Leroy stands and folds his blanket.

"She pumped you like a barnyard hand pump, you idjit. You just kept gushing who we are, where we're from, where we're headed. If that ain't information, then what is it?"

"I was just being sociable to a nun. That's all."

"Well, mister sociable, what was her name? What mission was she from? Who was the priest she was going to see? Where is she headed? I ain't real sure she was a she."

"Whoa, whoa, whoa, Rafe. We all saw her come in here with her nun dress and hood, a beaded belt with danglin' cross, and a white collar." Raylin sits on the log.

"That's all window dressin'. It don't make a she a she. Didn't her voice seem awful low to you? She waltzed right in here amongs't men and took over the conversation. She sits down cross-legged. When ever did you see a nun do that? Those mule eared boots ain't for women."

"Ain't no reason a woman can't wear boots." Raylin continues sharpening his blade.

"What good does it do to argue with you? Rooster and you up and ride off for days and then turn up again. I can't hardly depend on you." Rafe kneels by the fire pit and pulls together kindling to start a fire. Soon the blaze begins, and he adds more wood.

"I do remember men dressin' like women during the war," mumbles Raylin. "Me and Richard signed up with the 12th Mississippi when the war started. I was only sixteen and I lied for him. After four years we mustered out at Appomattox. Along the way, Richard lost his mind and became Rooster. After Sharpsburg, Gettysburg, Spotsylvania, Cold Harbor, and the trenches of Petersburg I seen men do all kinds of strange things. Some wore dresses, shawls, kerchiefs, and women's hats. They danced around and giggled like little girls. Then we lined up shoulder to shoulder and screamed that God-awful Rebel yell and ran straight into Yankee cannons and rifles. That's all I have to say about that."

Rafe looks at the bearlike man sitting on the log with tears etching a route down his cheeks into his beard.

Beside him Rooster stands and smiles in a manner that lights up his face. His entire countenance changes to self-assured, confident, and it appears to Rafe the man has lost five years. He appears alert and conversant. With eyes sparkling and a wide engaging grin that seems to pull a person toward him, Rooster says, "I'll take care of my big brother."

When Rooster finishes speaking, it's as if a curtain closes and he squats and returns to clucking quietly.

Standing awestruck, Rafe finally breaks the spell and kicks the frying pan toward Leroy. "Grab the bacon out of the grub bag and fry up some for breakfast."

He walks into the tall prairie grass to relieve himself.

It is a shout and scream that shakes the point rider out of his reverie, plodding along in front of the bell steer. Over the hill in front of him ride seven Indian braves. Three wear leather shirts, and four are shirtless. All have long leather leggings, and they wave their lances and coup sticks. Benjamin Johns snaps alert and eases back into the herd moving up around him. A quick glance over his shoulder, and he sees Angus Tremain gallop toward the front of the herd.

Benjamin watches Angus stop and talk with the Indians. He catches broken phrases of English and sees a lot of sign language.

Angus turns and motions Benjamin forward.

"Go get Chadbourne and tell him to get up here right now."

"Yes, Boss, on my way." Benjamin kicks his horse into a gallop toward Dr. Wisenheimer's wagon.

"Chad, you better get up," says Isaac as he watches Benjamin approach the wagon. "Looks like we have company coming."

Chad stretches and rises from the pallet he piled up on the wagon tailgate. He pulls his horse over to him and steps into the saddle. He's mounted as Benjamin races up to the wagon.

"Mister Chad, the Boss needs to see you. We've got Indians."

"Well, let's go Benjamin. Can't keep the neighbors waiting."

They gallop to the front of the herd and join Angus.

"What have you got on your hands, Angus?" asks Chad riding up.

"Benjamin, start turning the herd into itself. Tell the swing riders to help."

"Yes, Boss."

"Chad, we've got friends that know you, it appears." Angus gestures to the seven Indians.

Chad looks at the riders and recognizes *Shikoba* among them.

"I know the tall one in the middle." Chad raises his hand in a peace sign to *Shikoba*. "Good to see you again."

"That's the one that keeps sayin' he wants to talk to the Coffee Man. I recalled you telling me about your passing the pot with the two Indians and figured he meant you."

"We talk about cattle now," says *Shikoba*. He points to a nearby hilltop. Everyone rides to the hill, dismounts, and begins a conversation.

The group is seated on the ground, and Chad turns to Angus.

"You know if you give him too many, he'll think there are more to be given, and if you give him too few, they'll steal the rest." Chad stands with his back to the group with Angus beside him.

"Yeah, I know. What's the right answer? They want ten beeves."

"How about we give him six now, and once we're over the Red Fork River, we'll leave four behind for him. That puts us out of Choctaw Territory and into Cherokee."

"What's to stop the Cherokee from doing the same thing?"

"Nothin'. It's just the cost of doin' business in Indian Territory. Maybe the Cherokee aren't as hungry."

"If we don't, they'll sneak up and scatter the herd and pick up what they want, won't they?"

"Yep. That's what I would do."

"Okay. You talk to the Choctaw. He seems to like you better."

"That's just because I'm a more likeable person than you, Angus."

With a snort of derision, Angus says, "Let's get this done with." He returns to the group and kneels on one knee.

Chad returns and says, "Trail boss says that you may have six beeves now and four after we cross the Red Fork."

Shikoba counters, "We take all ten now. No need to wait."

"This dealing is like drinking coffee, *Shikoba*. If we give up ten beeves now, that's like drinking black coffee. It leaves us bitter. If we do six now and four after crossing the river, it's like adding sugar and makin' everythin' sweeter."

"You know we can take all now."

"I know you can try. Some of your people and some of mine will pay a high price for beef. Are you willing to pay the price when you can get what you're asking for in two steps?"

With a fleeting smile, *Shikoba* answers, "You should have been a Choctaw, Coffee Man. Will accept six now and four at river."

"I'll have two of my boys cut out six beeves and drive them to your camp. Leave a brave behind to lead them."

"Good. We go. Will see you at river." The Indians rise, and six ride away, leaving behind the seventh as a guide.

Angus and Chad walk away, mount, and ride back toward the herd.

"Better get Benjamin Johns and Lamont Becker to cut six from the drags and push them to where that Indian directs," says Chad.

"Why those two drovers?" asks Angus.

"Because Benjamin will follow through and make sure Lamont does so as well."

"All right, I'll tell them, and then we'll start the herd movin'." Angus reins his horse toward the chuckwagon while Chad heads toward Isaac's wagon.

Cutting out the six cows from the drags isn't a tough job but pushing them away from the herd requires Benjamin to use the end of his lariat to slap their tail ends and his horse to nudge the reluctant cows. They don't want to leave. Another cowboy, Lamont, comes to help. Finally, both cowboys and the cattle are following the lead of the Indian brave.

"Why are we doing this?" asks Lamont.

"Because the Boss said to. Ain't that enough for you?" Benjamin looks at his partner, the same age, same sandy hair, and brown eyes, except Lamont is almost rail thin. He has to pull his chaps almost together in back to keep them from slipping down over his non-existent hips. Since they are headed out, they've strapped on their holsters and pistols. Lamont's revolver looks like a cannon compared to his size.

"When are you gonna start puttin' some meat on your bones?" asks Benjamin. "You almost look like a scarecrow."

"Why, I eat all the time. The grub on this drive is great. Ol' Manolito knows how to fix things just fine."

Benjamin knows Lamont comes from a family of three

other brothers and four sisters. He saw the Boss give Lamont's widowed mom part of his wages before they left on the drive. *I don't think Lamont knows what the Boss did. Don't know what he'd think about it, but his mom was sure appreciative. She cried and cried.*

"Why's the Boss givin' injuns beeves?" asks Lamont.

"So they don't take more or stampede the herd. Don't you get that?"

"Don't know that I ever thought about it. It's my first drive you know."

"Mine too, but I heard the Boss and Mister Chad talkin' about makin' a deal with the Indians. He said this is the 'cost of doin' business.'"

"What's to keep the injuns from takin' more any time they want?"

"Trust."

"With the injuns? Come on, get serious."

"Mister Chad is dead set that Indians keep their word. He says it's white folks you can't ever turn your back on."

"Go on, get out."

"Truth. I heard him say it."

"Where are we following this injun to?"

"A camp. Then we'll catch up with the herd."

"You mean you volunteered me to ride into an injun camp with you? Are you loco or just crazy?"

"That's the deal. We drive these beeves to the camp and then leave. In and out."

"With or without our scalps?"

"As Mister Chad tells the Boss, 'Don't worry about the little things.'"

"You remember to repeat that to me when we're back with

the herd. Okay?"

"I'll try to remember. Look over there. We got a couple of heifers blazin' their own trail." Lamont spurs after the two straying beeves.

It's been all day and turning dusk when the cowboys top a rise and look into the creek bottom at the base of the hill. Beside the wooded thicket, they see six teepees arranged in a circular pattern, wooden hanging racks, rough wood tables and stands holding water bags. Women and children wander around the camp. Ten horses graze in the grass a short distance from the village.

Their Indian guide points at the camp, and Benjamin and Lamont push the cattle over the hilltop toward the village.

Almost as if they spring from the ground, eight mounted Indians race toward them.

"Are we gonna die, Benjamin?" asks Lamont. "They're comin' right at us."

"Keep your head, push the cattle, and don't touch your firearm," says Benjamin.

"Okay, but my momma ain't gonna be happy if you go and get me killed."

"The Boss and Mister Chad said to just go, do our job, and leave. That's what we'll do."

The Indian riders surround the cattle and cowboys, whooping and hollering as they usher the herd toward the camp. Benjamin spots a rope corral in a grassy spot beside the camp and knows that's where the cattle need to go. He motions Lamont, and they drive the six beeves into the corral, dismount, and tie the rope enclosure closed.

The women and children rush out to watch the milling cattle.

A tall Indian rides toward the two cowboys.

"I am called *Shikoba*."

"I'm Benjamin and my pardner is Lamont." Benjamin steps from his saddle and loosens his horse's cinch to give it a chance to blow.

"You've done what Coffee Man promised. That is good."

"Yes, sir. We followed orders from our boss and Mister Chad. Are we free to go?"

"You may leave whenever you wish. Before you leave, come to my teepee. I have a gift for Coffee Man."

Benjamin turns to Lamont. "We're good to go. I've got to follow this Indian to get something. I'll meet you on top of the hill. Go scout someplace to bed down for tonight. I don't want to ride around out here in the dark."

"All right. I'll head back the way we came and find us a spot. Watch for the campfire." Lamont spurs his horse uphill, riding to the summit. He turns and waves at Benjamin before disappearing over the top.

Benjamin walks his horse toward the teepee where the tall Indian waits. When he stops before the teepee, *Shikoba* reaches into a canvas bag he holds and pulls out a new white enamel coffee pot. He holds it out for Benjamin to see.

"Give to Coffee Man. Tell him is time to throw away old pot." He puts the item back in the sack and hands it to Benjamin.

Benjamin ties the sack to his saddle horn, tightens the cinch, and steps into his saddle.

"I'll tell him. Goodbye." He rides out of the village and climbs the hill. At the top, he turns and waves.

The tall Indian waves back.

Dark is settling fast as Benjamin trots back along the trail the cattle made through the grassy prairie. He's looking for the flicker of a campfire and sees only darkness.

Where's Lamont? I should be seein' a fire. He couldn't have gone that far.

Standing in his stirrups, Benjamin sweeps the landscape all around. The only glimmer of light is from stars sparkling above him.

No campfire.

12

TRIBULATION

ANOTHER BOTTLE FLIES OUT THE BACK OF THE wagon and shatters into pieces as it strikes the ground. The amber liquid inside quickly soaks into the prairie.

Isaac leans across the driver's seat and into the enclosed wagon, talking loudly. "All right Abigail. All right. We'll talk with Chad and Angus; only don't throw out another bottle of elixir. I don't have that many left, and Abilene is a long way away."

Chad rides toward the wagon and watches bottles fly out the back. He hears Isaac's pleading and stops at the front of the wagon.

"Seems you've got a problem with Miss Abigail, Isaac." He pulls his left foot from the stirrup and hooks his leg around the saddle horn. Leaning forward, he smiles.

"You've got to get Angus to free her movements from just this wagon. She's going to destroy my inventory one bottle at a time."

"You wanted her to go with us. Now you've got to deal with her."

"We don't have a choice. Taking her back to Red River Station isn't an option. You know that, so don't make this all my fault."

Chad chuckles lightly. "I know it's not just your doin'. You gather up the *she devil,* and we'll go to the chuckwagon and meet with Angus."

"Abigail, Abigail, do you hear?" says Isaac.

Around from the back of the steps appears Abigail. She straightens her skirt and hair.

"It's about time someone sees the error of his ways and rectifies this untenable situation."

Chad undrapes his leg from around the saddle horn and places his boot back in its stirrup.

"I still am not real sure what she says, but if she means we'll find a way to fix things, then she's right. I'm heading for the chuckwagon." He reins his horse toward the campfire.

Leaping down from the wagon seat, Isaac reaches for Abigail's arm, helps her step down, and together they follow Chad.

The four lounging cowboys jump to their feet and hold their hats in their hands. Angus watches their actions and looks over his shoulder. Abigail, Isaac, and Chad approach the campfire.

He rises and turns to face them.

"You know you're out of bounds."

"Yes, Angus, she knows. Let's talk," says Chad stepping into the fire circle and sitting on a log beside the fire. The cowboys gather their gear and move from the circle. Isaac cleans a spot on the log with his handkerchief and Abigail takes a seat.

Angus sits down.

"Well, let's hear it. What's brought this about?"

Manolito passes out cups for coffee.

"We've been a few weeks on the trail now, and Miss Abigail has taken her confinement without argument. The boys have seen her, and she ain't caused any ruckus. It's about time to turn her loose," says Chad.

"Turn her loose, you say." Angus stretches out his legs in front of him.

"Yes, Mister Tremain. I've abided by your demands, but now I feel like I'm a prisoner and will no longer be confined." Abigail brushes loose strands of hair from her face.

"Well, ain't that just the be all? I was of a mind to lift my decision, but I sure don't like being told to do something. How about if you was to ask, politely like?"

Chad watches Abigail with a smirk. *Sometimes Angus likes yankin' the rope just a little. Let's see if Abigail takes his bait or sees through him.*

Abigail stands and slowly walks past the campfire. She turns and looks directly at Angus and pauses. *He's playing with me. I don't like being exploited. If I explode, he can demand my incarceration continues. If I give in and ask him, he wins. How can I achieve success without losing face?*

Abigail replies, "If pots and pans are banged and rattled at night, could that cause trouble? Perhaps breaking bottles

142

unexpectedly might cause unexpected results. What are your thoughts, Mister Tremain?"

Angus' brow furrows as he glares at Abigail. "There ain't nothin' funny in what you're saying, ma'am. With a flighty herd those things mean trouble."

"It would be a shame to have someone restricted to a point that something like that might just happen, wouldn't it?"

Chad slips back off the log. *She's a good one. Got ol' Angus on the ropes. If he says she stays captive, anything could happen. He loses. If he gives her freedom, he loses face unless he makes it out to be his idea. That's one quick-thinkin' gal.*

Angus stands and tucks in his shirt. "I've been thinkin' it's time you're free to roam. Consider confinement lifted." He walks toward the horses's picket line.

Well, I've seen Angus bulldogged by one of the best. That girl is a worthy opponent. I hope Isaac knows what he is tanglin' with in this female. She's gritty. Chad stands and follows Angus to the horses.

Isaac pours another cup of coffee for Abigail and himself as they remain seated by the campfire.

Riding toward the herd, Chad knows better than bring up the confrontation with Abigail. They ride in silence until Angus speaks.

"Been long enough for Benjamin and Lamont to be back."

With a twinge of anxiety, Chad replies, "I'll take Isaac and backtrack to find them. Hopefully, they're just slow catching up."

"You do that. We're fixin' to cross the Red Fork in another day and need everybody to get across. Go get 'em."

Chad pulls the reins on his horse as he heads back to get Isaac.

Benjamin circles around again, beginning another circuit, attempting to locate tracks to follow.

Where is Lamont? He can't have gone far and why aren't there tracks to follow?

He's crossed any number of unshod trails, but so far, no shod tracks beside his.

Suddenly, he stops, slides from his saddle, and gently brushes aside ground cover.

There, there's a track pointing north.

Afoot, he leads his horse as he continues to move in that direction, looking for another impression in the ground.

Another, over there.

He brushes aside scrub brush.

And, another. I've got a trail now.

He flings himself into his saddle, and leaning over to study the ground, he kicks his horse into a fast walk.

There are at least two riders, maybe three. They are real careful about leaving a trail.

Benjamin moves forward tracking up and down the rolling hills.

"I'm a damn fool, damn fool," says Chad loping along with Isaac beside him. Their horses carry them away from the herd. They are headed toward the location where Benjamin and Lamont drove the six cattle.

"Maybe there is nothing to worry about. They could just be

taking their time," replies Isaac.

"Or maybe, by my not paying attention, we've got another situation. I was stupid to take my mind off that killer. When you quit payin' attention out here, something dies."

"You had Miss Abigail to worry about."

"Exactly. I took my mind off what was important and now I fear we're headin' toward a problem."

"Well, I choose to be optimistic and know we will find our cowboys larking along."

"Optimist or pessimist don't make no never mind. Something still dies."

Chad kicks his horse into a faster lope and Isaac spurs to keep up.

Benjamin pulls his horse to a stop. On the horizon, he spots birds slowly circling.

Buzzards.

He kicks his horse into a flat-out run.

Chad sees the buzzards in the distance and points them out to Isaac.

"Over there, see them circling? We've got trouble."

Spurring his horse, Chad leans over its neck as the animal springs into a ground-gulping gallop.

Topping the rise, Chad looks into the shallow valley between two ridges. A horse stands beside a figure sprawled on the ground. Glancing up, he spots another rider approaching from over a hill on the far side of the valley.

It's Benjamin, I recognize the blaze-faced horse. Where's he been? What's in the valley?

Isaac pulls up beside Chad.

"Who's down there?" He points toward the valley. "Look, another rider is coming toward us."

"Yep, it's Benjamin, and I believe I know who's down in the valley. Let's get there."

Chad leads Isaac down the slope toward the prone figure. Reaching the tethered horse, he slips from his saddle and walks toward the body on the ground. Behind him Isaac is dismounted and vomiting. The body on the ground is staked out spread eagle with what appears to be hundreds of stab wounds. The throat is sliced with such brutality it almost severs the head. A pool of blood surrounds the body, and Chad recognizes the victim. It's Lamont.

Isaac stands beside his horse, using the saddle to steady himself.

"Who would do something like this? Why do it to Lamont?"

"Only an animal kills like this. No, I'm wrong. Animals don't even do this. Only some deranged human kills like this." Chad dismounts and stands beside the body.

"Why pick on these young boys?"

"This creature finds real pleasure in inflicting pain and torture on young men. There's something twisted here, and I don't know what it is."

"I thought we were finished with this fiend," Isaac says.

If I was a half-way decent detective, maybe we would be, but so far I'm only ridin' drag on this killer. He or she is ahead of me at every turn. "We'll not be finished until we find him and put an end to him." Chad turns and walks to Lamont's horse that stands ground tied beside the body.

"What about Benjamin?" Isaac points at the rapidly approaching rider.

"Go, stop him before he gets here."

Isaac steps into his saddle and rides quickly to intercept Benjamin.

Chad pulls the slicker from behind the saddle on Lamont's horse. He covers the body, pulls his knife and cuts the leather straps tying it to the ground. Carefully he rolls Lamont's body onto the slicker, picks it up, and drapes it across the standing horse.

Benjamin and Isaac ride up.

"It's Lamont, ain't it?"

"Yep. He's dead. Was tortured. Don't know a nice way to say it," says Chad.

"I let him ride ahead. The Indian chief called me back to give me something for you. I figured I could catch up with Lamont. He said he'd stop and set up camp, start a fire."

"I want you and Isaac to start back to camp. I've got some lookin' around to do."

"You sure you want to ride with me, Mister Isaac. It appears I'm some kind of Jonah."

"You are definitely no Jonah, Benjamin. I'll gladly ride with you. Will you be all right out here, Chad?"

"I'm fine. I want to look around before we lose the light. This wasn't done by some ghost, so there has to be signs of him somewhere." *If there's anything to find, I'm going to find it*

147

and finish this. It's gone on too long, and too many good boys have died.

"Very well. We will leave but expect you to follow very soon." Isaac takes the reins of Lamont's horse as he and Benjamin ride toward the herd.

Chad walks slowly around the area where Lamont was staked. Brushing aside ground clutter he finds boot prints sunk into the earth. *This thing ain't no light weight to make prints like that.*

Chad widens his circle searching for more clues. He stops when he finds horse tracks. *A horse stood here. The depths of the hoof prints tell me that it had a rider. What was he waiting for? Lamont to die? Benjamin to catch up? What?*

Chad has a feeling, a sixth-sense, that somebody or something is watching him as he surveys the area where Lamont was staked out. Pausing, he stands and looks around. Nothing is visible on the surrounding hilltops or from the swales around him.

It's out there, and I know it has eyes on me. I can feel them. Show me where you're at, you monster. Just show me, and it's your last day alive.

Chad turns to his horse and steps into his saddle. He heads toward the herd.

As the last light fades over the horizon, Chad spots a lone figure in the distance riding parallel to him. It's too dark to make out any details, just a lone figure on horseback keeping its distance. Chad slides his rifle from its scabbard, laying it across his saddle's pommel.

It's him. How can I get to him without his slippin' away? He's too far to get a good look or a shot. He's taunting me, wants me to know he's there. Come closer, damned you, and you're dead.

A sudden flash grabs Chad's attention. Lightning strikes on the horizon, and Chad feels a buzz in the air tingle the hair of his arms. Thunder rolls across the prairie, sounding like cannon fire. His horse shudders, and he tightly holds the reins as he strokes the animal's neck for reassurance. Dark clouds mass in front of the setting sun, and Chad watches multiple lightning strikes pound the ground and dance through the clouds.

13

STAMPEDE

THE CAMPFIRE BURNS BRIGHTLY AGAINST THE DARK, black, massed clouds that roll across the prairie. Lightening spits and flashes. Deep, ominous thunder rolls, peal after peal, and feels like it bounces along the ground. The wind velocity picks up and begins to whine. Its banshee sound is enough to put nerves on edge.

Chad sees Manolito hustling around the fire, putting away cooking utensils. Isaac and Abigail help. Not one cowboy is in the camp as he rides up.

Angus has all the boys with the herd, keeping the cattle quiet and in check. This 'toad strangler' is going to test 'em. Hope Russell has the remuda ready to run. One noise, one sound is enough to break the herd loose.

Isaac pauses as he sees Chad ride up to the chuckwagon.

"We were getting concerned. You've taken your time to get back."

"Yep, had to check for clues and then was stalked by the killer on my way here."

"He's here? The killer is here?"

"Close. He left me a few miles back. What about Lamont?"

"Angus and the boys buried him on the hill behind us. Then the storm started kicking up, and everyone turned to taking care of the herd."

"Glad to hear the boy's properly buried. I'm goin' to find Angus. Stick close to your wagon. When Manolito moves out, keep right with him. He knows what to do."

"Abigail sang a song over Lamont, made everyone feel a little better. All the boys thanked her."

"That was nice of her. Keep her close to you. It's goin' to get rough before it gets better tonight."

Chad turns toward the herd when a bolt of lightning strikes close by, and the sky begins dumping hail.

Rain pummels down, beating on everything it strikes. Chad manages to slip on his slicker, but water runs down over the collar soaking him. His hat runs a river of water off the brim. He sees Angus moving beside the herd and rides to him.

"You think they'll break?" he shouts over the wind.

"They're antsy enough. Got a group milling around in the middle every time the lightening snaps. If they bolt, all hell will break loose." Angus motions to a cowboy to push straying cows back to the herd.

"Glad you got Lamont buried before this hit."

"Just in time. Now, we got our hands full."

"What are you goin' to do if they bolt?"

"Let 'em run. We ain't about to stop them in this storm. Best we can hope is they'll run themselves out without killin' too many."

"Russell got the remuda far enough away to hold them?"

"Hope so. Horses run forever, and gathering them up takes a lot more time."

"I'm gettin' to the top of that hill over there to keep an eye on trouble spots."

"You do that, I'm headin' over to help tighten' the bunch up."

Chad rides past the herd to the hilltop when he sees bluish shimmery tendrils of light dance and skip across the cattles' long horns.

Oh, hell, they're gonna break. St. Elmo's fire is dancin' and lightening' is close.

In the next moment, three lightning bolts hit the ground simultaneously beside the herd.

In full panic, the longhorns in the middle break and explode into full-out running to escape the lightening.

They sweep up other cattle like a cyclone as they push them in an onrush like leaves driven by a whirlwind. Soon the night is full of the sounds of cannon-fire thunder, shrieking wind, crackling lightening, and clacking of horns as the cattle stampede. Twenty-five hundred beeves string out across the prairie in a terrified rush.

From the hilltop, Chad watches the cowboys dig their heels into their ponies as they race with the stampede.

There's no stoppin' them now. They got to run off the fright; in a while we can start turning the leaders into the center and stop the run. Right now, everybody needs to hold on and keep from running into a ravine or wash and getting trampled.

Chad races off the hill to the front of the herd and gallops through the rain avoiding the horns of terrified cattle. He gives the reins to his horse knowing it can find its way better than he can. If his horse goes down, there's nothing to keep tons of cattle from running over him.

Benjamin races along with the cattle as Chad dashes alongside of him.

"Give your horse its head," he hollers to Benjamin. "Keep out in front, let's give them a few more miles, and then we'll start turning them."

Benjamin nods his head, slushing water from his hat as the rain continues to beat down on men and beasts.

Thank God for open prairie to run across. Woods or ravines would kill a bunch. Another mile or so and we'll turn them. Chad leans low across his horse's neck to keep from overbalancing the running animal.

The pounding of hooves sends vibrations through the ground that Chad feels beneath his horse. Cattle from fright, instinct, panic, or simple mass mentality run at breakneck speed into the dark night, oblivious to anything around them. Their single motivation is to run as long, hard, and fast as possible.

Chad knows that animals will die, be trampled, or break limbs. His overwhelming concern is that the cowboys remain clear of the panic-stricken animals and stay alive while trying to keep them from scattering too far. The hours of the night pass as men, horses, and cattle burn adrenalin and spend their strength and stamina.

The rain slackens, and the lightening marches across the

prairie away from the herd. The wind and thunder die away and dissipate.

Chad motions for Benjamin to begin turning the stampede. Two more cowboys join them, and together they move the lead cattle into a milling circle that starts consuming the momentum from the runaway animals. As the strung-out herd begins compressing into a swirling circle, their remaining energy evaporates, and soon they walk around and around, slowing down and recovering their wind.

"Keep 'em turning," shouts Chad. "Anybody seen Angus?"

"He's ridin' drag at the end, catchin' up as many strays as he can," shouts a skinny cowboy.

"Stay on top of this bunch and keep turning 'em. I'm goin' back to find Angus."

"Want me to go with you?" asks Benjamin.

"You stay here and take charge of the operation. You did well tonight. I'll be back." Chad turns and rides past milling cattle.

Chad rides back along the worn path of churned-up sod created by the stampede. The morning sun creeps over the horizon as he passes the sodden mass of fatigued cattle stumbling along. Beside the herd, he passes drenched cowboys with their heads hanging down on their chests as they loll along physically and emotionally spent. A few raise their heads and nod as Chad passes. Others continue to drift along unaware of his presence.

It's been a hard night, but they've lived through it.

Chad passes the end of the herd without seeing Angus. He

continues to follow the trail and soon sees a figure walking his direction. Spurring his worn-out horse, he quickly moves to the mud-caked man.

"You decide to get down and roll in the mud?" Chad stops his horse and looks at Angus.

"I figured I'd just wear a little of the territory on me for a while." Angus wipes the mud from his face. "It would be funny if it didn't cost me a right fine horse to get this way."

"What happened?"

"Was followin' the herd, chasin' up a stray steer when it twisted back and tried to hook my horse with its horn. My cayuse jumped out of the way, and both front legs stuck in a muddy bog. They snapped like a tree branch breakin'. It was a God-awful sound. The horse thrashin' around on the ground, screamin' in pain, the rain, lightening, thunder…I shot him. Been stompin' along out here, followin' y'all ever since. Is everybody okay?"

"Benjamin and the boys have circled the herd. It's millin' around a few miles ahead. Looks like everyone is accounted for. We're lucky. Come on. Get aboard." Chad kicks his left boot out of its stirrup and makes room for Angus to climb up behind him.

Angus settles behind Chad's saddle, wrapping an arm around his waist.

"When the sun's up, we'll dry things out and then start roundin' up strays. I'll send a couple of boys back to gather my saddle and gear."

"Let's go find Manolito. I could use some coffee and grub. It's been a long night," says Chad.

"I'm with you, Amigo. We survived another one."

14

DECISION

CHAD SITS ASTRIDE HIS HORSE. HIS ARMS ARE CROSSED and resting on the saddle horn.

"Not bad work gettin' to this point in six days."

Isaac sits beside him on his horse, watching the cowboys push cattle away from the river.

"Four days to round up all the strays and move the herd to the Red Fork River, a day's rest, and today the herd is pushed over. So, that is making good time?"

"Mighty fine time with nobody hurt or lost in the process."

"What about the twenty-five cows killed in the stampede?"

"That's the cost of doin' business."

"Is that what the boys are doing holding those four beeves from crossing the river? The cost of doing business?"

"Yep. Look up on the hill back aways."

Isaac spots four Indians sitting on their ponies, watching the cowboy circle the four longhorns.

"They're makin' sure our word is good," says Chad. He points at the Indians riding down toward the river. Taking his hat off, he waves it back and forth over his head as he stands in his stirrups. The cowboy across the river spots Chad, takes his hat off, waves it in response, turns his horse, lopes it to the river, and crosses.

"We're good to go now?" asks Isaac.

"Yep. We're on the short end of the trail now. A few more days to the Arkansas River, cross it, and make a straight run to Abilene. I'd say we're only two weeks away."

"Can we catch up with Manolito and Abigail now? I know they are making peach cobbler for dinner. If we don't get there, the boys will lick the Dutch oven clean."

"Let's ride then." Chad tugs the reins on his horse and spurs it into an easy lope. Isaac keeps up with him.

"I want to run some things past you while we're ridin'," says Chad.

"About the killings?"

"Yep."

"What are you thinking?"

"I'm thinkin' we're dealin' with some real deranged mind. Somethin' traumatic or altering has warped the person."

"Okay. A life or death issue? Murder? War? What?"

"We've got lots of men back from the war. They saw a lot, and most of it wasn't good. It could have bent some minds. You know what I mean?"

"Okay. Say that is it. Why choose only boys to kill?"

"Think about the war. Who was killed on the battlefields? Sixteen to twenty-five-year-old boys for the most part. Oh, there were older cusses as the war went on, but for the most part, boys died. Thousands of them."

"So, you are proposing this fiend is still fighting the war?"

"That, or just can't let it go. His mind is warped about it."

"Interesting idea. What else do you have?"

The cowboy, after crossing the river, passes Chad and Isaac with a wave.

"He's going for peach cobbler. We're going to miss out." Isaac urges his horse into a faster lope. Chad keeps pace.

"After lookin' around all the kill sites, it appears the work is done by one person. The shod prints indicate it. Also, the weight is only one rider."

"How do you know that?"

"The depth the horseshoe cuts into the sod."

"Okay. What else?"

"Where Bucky and Lamont were killed, there was only one set of boot prints beside the boys."

"Only one?"

"Yep. Both sets had the same worn heel on the right foot."

"One person, right?"

"That's all that stalked me from Lamont's murder site."

"All right, mister detective, we are looking for one dark clad, deranged person, working alone, with one worn right boot heel. Is that it?"

"That's all I've got to work with right now."

"Great. Now where do we find this person?" Isaac sweeps his arm around the prairie.

"Out here, somewhere."

Chad points at the rapidly disappearing cowboy. "You know, he's gonna be eatin' my share of that peach cobbler." He spurs his horse into a ground-covering gallop.

Surprised by Chad's action, Isaac sits momentarily watching him speed away. Recovering, he spurs his horse to catch up.

The cowboy stands over the Dutch oven and uses his spoon to scrape out the last bit of peach cobbler crust stuck to the bottom. Two boys walk toward the soapy tub of water, licking their plates before dropping them into the suds.

"Looks like your cobbler is a real success." Chad looks at Abigail.

"Manolito is a wizard at putting together something out of nothing. I marvel at his talent. Yes, the cobbler hits the spot, but with these boys, as hungry as they are, they will eat anything."

"It's been a hard fought few days since the stampede. This cobbler is a real treat."

"Is it much farther to Abilene?"

"Isaac and I were speculating that another couple of weeks should put us at the loading pens."

"I'll be glad when we are there. It is a hard life out here. How foolish I was to think I could traverse this trail alone. Thank you for all you have done for me."

"Not me, Miss Abigail. This drive is Angus' responsibility. He's the one who picked you up."

"Aside from our rocky start and my confinement, we seem to have settled on toleration. He has been nothing short of a gentleman."

"Don't let him hear that. His head will swell up, and he'd not be able to wear his hat."

Abigail, laughing aloud a soft happy sound, rises and moves to help Manolito clean up and wash dishes.

"She is something, isn't she?" Isaac focuses on Abigail's activity.

"That she is, Isaac. By the way, what happened with y'all and the storm?" Chad pushes his hat back on his head.

"Well, we followed Manolito's directions, as you told us to do. We pulled the wagons together on the highest hill beside the camp just before the herd took off. Manolito said that we should stay put because the cowboys would come looking for us after the storm."

"He's right. You wanderin' around amongst stampeding animals is a genuine mistake."

"He hobbled his mules, as I did mine, and went inside the chuckwagon out of the elements. Abigail retreated from the weather into my wagon. I sat on the driver's seat wrapped in a serape Manolito gave me, trying to keep as dry as possible and failing miserably."

"So, you sat there through the storm?"

"Not exactly."

"What's *not exactly* mean?"

"Shortly, Abigail opened the door on my wagon and told me to come inside."

"Oh."

"Now, see here my good man. There was nothing amiss or questionable that occurred. She simply asked me in out of the inclement weather." Isaac glares at Chad.

"Okay. Okay. Nothing happened."

"What did happen was that we talked for the longest time about our lives, interests, and plans. We discovered how much alike we are in many ways and the many things we have in common. Of course, I did comfort her when the storm howled its worst."

"Comforted?"

"Why must you imply the tawdry? She is a very Victorian lady, and I respect her. No. I love her. There, I've said it. Satisfied?"

"Well, well, well, Doctor Wisenheimer, I believe you are in the clutches of Lady Love. What about Abigail? How does she feel?"

"From our conversation and the comforting we gave each other, I believe she reciprocates my feelings."

"How's she feel about your being a snake-oil salesman?"

"If I've told you once, I've told you a hundred times. I sell medicinal elixirs. What is so difficult about that to understand?"

"Oh, maybe because your elixirs get you chased out of almost every town you've been in."

"Narrow-minded people who do not appreciate what is done for them."

"Be that as it may, you haven't answered my question. What does Abigail think about your occupation?"

"I am a trained pharmacist, and she is an educator. Abilene should hold some promises for new beginnings."

"Now then, that wasn't too difficult. A worthy trade and a new location should pay off for you. Are you pursuing the new beginning with Abigail?"

"Certainly. Without her, there is no new beginning."

"Well said, Isaac. Well said. I applaud your decision. When we reach Abilene, I'll release you from your commitment to me, and you are free to start anew. Deal?"

"That has been assumed from the beginning."

"In the meantime, we have a killer to catch. Let's go to work." Chad rises, dumps his dish in the washtub, tips his hat to Abigail, and walks toward the picket line to claim his horse. Isaac hustles to keep up, giving Abigail a swift kiss on the cheek in passing.

Abigail stands beside the campfire, drying towel in hand, watching both men depart.

15

LAST RIVER

FOUR RIDERS SIT ON THEIR HORSES BESIDE THE swollen Arkansas River. Their pack mule stands patiently behind them. Branches, tree trunks, brush, and debris washed from upriver sweep past. The water crests at the edge of the banks, threatening to burst over the top and flood the prairie.

"We've beat the herd to the river, but that damned storm has kicked up this mess." Rafe leans back in his saddle.

"Yeah, that means we sit here trapped between the water and the cattle." Raylin shrugs his shoulders, trying to get more comfortable.

"Maybe we need to find a place back in the hills to camp and get off the flat. What'd you think?" asks Leroy.

"I think we'll stay here and wait for the water to drop.

Between here and Abilene we'll need to take the herd. Catchin' them boys crossin' the river will be the best time. After they get almost all the cattle over, we'll hit 'em. They won't see it comin'."

"They still outgun us Rafe. Why not hit 'em from a distance with our rifles?" Leroy looks to Raylin for support.

"Because you can't hit the broadside of a barn, you idjit. That's why."

"I think you're fixin' to get us killed." Leroy rides to the edge of the bank and watches the water spin and swirl as it rushes past.

Rooster rides closer to his brother and looks with frightened eyes at the rushing current.

"Yeah. I know. You don't like this do you? But, it ain't nothin' but water." Raylin rides to the edge of the bank to show Rooster there's nothing to fear.

Rafe watches in shock as the bank under Raylin's horse gives away and the animal slides into the rushing water. To keep from going into the river with the horse, Raylin leaps from his saddle into the brush on the shoreline. He slides into the water and suddenly erupts from the vegetation. He's covered with snakes. One hangs from his cheek, another is attached to his neck, two more sink their fangs into his arms, and two black snakes hang from his torso. He flails and snatches at the dangling reptiles.

"Oh hell, water moccasins. Get them off him," shouts Rafe jumping from his saddle and trying to get to Raylin without being bitten. He grabs a tree limb and beats at the poisonous snakes in an attempt to kill them.

Raylin lies on the riverbank, gasping for air. His body quivers and shakes as the snakes slide over and off of him, heading back for the water.

"My brother, my brother," wails Rooster. "Help my brother."

With a sudden intake of breath, Raylin slowly exhales and lies still.

Rooster slides from his saddle and kneels beside Raylin.

"Kill 'em. Kill 'em all." Pulling his pistol, Rooster rushes to the waterline and fires repeatedly at the snakes in the brush. "Die, damn you, die."

A submerged tree suddenly pops to the surface of the river. Its scraggly roots jut out in every direction. They've been sharpened from rubbing on river rocks and the banks. Rooster stands on the riverbank with his back to the tree adrift in the boiling current.

"Rooster, look out," shouts Rafe.

Spinning around, Rooster sees the roots an instant before a sharpened point pierces his chest and shoves its way through his body. The tree doesn't stop. The force of the water's current lifts Rooster, impaled on the root, and continues its surge downstream.

Leroy fights to control his horse. The escaping snakes slipped around its feet and the horse twists and shies from side to side. Rafe see its white-eyed fear. The horse rears to escape the reptiles. Stumbling, it slips on the muddy bank and the steed's rear legs slide, flipping the animal over onto its back. Leroy doesn't have time to react and jump clear. Clinging to the saddle horn, the entire weight of the horse slams him into the ground. Rafe hears crunching sounds and knows Leroy's body is broken. The horse shifts around trying to regain its footing, only grinding Leroy deeper into the ground.

Avoiding the staggering horse, Rafe rushes over and kneels beside Leroy. He sees a blossom of spreading scarlet cover Leroy's chest.

"Lie still. Don't move."

"He kilt me, didn't he?" Blood bubbles in Leroy's mouth. "My damned horse kilt me."

"I don't know what I can do, Leroy. Just lie still." Frantically, Rafe looks around for anything to give Leroy some relief.

"I told you we ought to gone to the hills," Leroy bubbles his words in blood, coughs, and lies still. His glassy stare straight ahead does not blink.

Rafe stands in shock. He looks at the scene around him.

All three gone, just like that. Damn the cattle, damn the Chisholm Trail, damn the prairie.

Quietly he turns to his horse, pulls his long duster around himself, mounts, and snatches up the halter rope of the mule. He kicks his horse into a slow walk. The mule trots behind.

There's got to be a crossing upriver.

The two cowboys stand beside the river and motion for Chad as he rides to the front of the herd. He stops beside them and steps from his saddle.

"What've you got, boys?"

"Looks like what's left of two men. Coyotes or wolves been after them some. One big guy looks like he's snake bit, all discolored and swoll' up. The other little guy's been crushed." The taller cowboy points at both men.

"Yeah. Birds been peckin' at them, too. Eyes and tongues are gone. Wait just a minute." Chad leans down to take a closer look, trying not to smell the decomposing bodies. "I think I've seen these two before."

"You seen them out here?" The smaller drover looks at the

bodies again.

"I sure have. They were part of a foursome that I snuck up on a while ago."

"What are they doin' here?"

"Dyin'," says Chad. "Grab a right leg on both of them, I want to see their boot heels."

Each cowboy grabs a leg and lifts the boot for Chad to examine.

"Nope. Not what I was hopin' for."

"What do we do with them, Chad?"

"Roll 'em over in that little ditch and pitch some dirt on 'em. That's the best we can do now. Gather up any possibles they might have on them. We'll turn the items into the marshal in Abilene in case anybody ever asks."

"Yes, sir." Both boys start moving the bodies.

Angus rides up to Chad.

"What'd you find?"

"Two no-goods that ain't goin' to bother nobody no more."

"Then that's good for us."

"Yeah, I believe that is good for us."

"I scouted up river a bit and found a narrow and shallow crossing. The river dropped considerable and I think we'll try to move the herd over tomorrow."

"What about quicksand. You know once water rises the pools stick around for a while."

"Yeah. Checked for that too. Looks clear. Let's go back and let everybody know we have one more river to cross tomorrow."

"You're the boss. Give the word."

Blowing on his cup of hot coffee, Chad sits with Isaac by the campfire. Manolito and Abigail are fixing biscuits in the Dutch oven for hungry cowboys coming in from changing shifts. Half the crew has already finished up their biscuits and beans, and they head out to watch the herd. The other half is heading in for grub and sack-time.

"So, the boots don't match the tracks?" Isaac throws more cow chips on the fire.

"Nope. Those two didn't do the killin'. Now, somebody with them maybe did or somebody else, but not them."

"Well, we're back to the beginning again. No leads."

"Been that way since the get go. If we keep the boys doubled up between here and Abilene we may make it all right. Then we'll have to see what happens in Abilene."

"Are you going to tell Angus?"

"Already have, and he agrees. We may double up shifts and some work longer to keep from leaving anyone alone, but it's just what has to happen. I'm workin' with the boys as well. You need to pick a shift too."

"All right. I'll let Abigail know what's going on."

"You're gonna fit real nice with her. Yes, sir, real nice."

"Is that the last bunch, Benjamin?" Chad points to twenty-five or so cows milling around the riverbank.

"Yep, Chad. That's the last bunch. They're headin' over now."

"The last river. Glad to be across. Seems like a long time ago when I pulled your soggy butt from a river, don't it?"

"Like ages ago, Chad. Thanks for never tellin' nobody. Don't know if Mister Angus would have me as 'top hand' if you did."

"Not to worry. You've earned every bit of bein' 'top hand.' You takin' us into Abilene?"

"Yes, sir. Mister Angus has me ridin' point the rest of the way. In a couple of days, he's goin' into Abilene before us to meet with the owner's representative and cattle buyer. He'll be back to let us know what holdin' pen we've got to drive the herd into."

"You'll do us proud, Benjamin."

"Are you still lookin' for that scum that killed Bucky and Lamont?"

"Yep. We're takin' precautions against anybody else bein' killed. Maybe the fiend will show up in Abilene. Only time will tell."

"Let me know if I can help you."

"You keep your head in the game of leadin' this drive, and I'll keep mine trying to find a killer. Okay?"

"Yes, sir."

Benjamin turns his horse and rides toward the gathering herd.

16

ABILENE

CHAD RIDES TOWARD ABILENE IN APPREHENSION OF the end of the trail. His last trip up the Chisholm Trail found the little village a rip-snorting, hell-raising, den of iniquity.

I don't know if Joseph McCoy really understood Texas cow-boys when he built the first cattle pens alongside the Kansas Pacific railroad in Abilene. When boys at the end of a drive are cut loose, it means that the better part of a year without comforts of a bed or a roof over his head to protect from the elements have to be made up for.

Chad approaches town from the south, riding up Cedar Street to its intersection with Texas Street. He sees the railroad ahead, and off to the east he spots a large three-story house, his destination...the Drovers Cottage.

The boys are ready to 'open up' after months of cows, storms, high water, chuckwagon grub, dust, and heat. Once the herd's sold and the boys draw their pay, stand back. Every sharpie and whore south of the railroad will be after them. Texas Street will roar. I hope Angus has a good long talk with them before cutting them loose.

Chad continues to ride north on Cedar before turning east on Texas Street. It's quiet now, too early in the morning. Only the drunks stir on the saloon porches as he passes.

Won't be long before our boys will rush into the stores along this street to purchase a new outfit of clothes, maybe fancy quilted-top tight-fitting dress boots and new Stetson hats. A bath, in a real tub, along with a shave in the barbershop will remove all the trail grime before putting on their new duds. I imagine some will be talked into gettin' new pistols as well.

Chad rides past the Alamo, the largest and most palatial of the twenty-seven saloons and eight gambling halls in Abilene. It stretches forty feet along Cedar Street. He remembers it well.

There are entrances on either end. Three double glass doors. Inside and along one wall, the bar is shinin' with polished brass fixtures and rails. The back bar reflects all the brightly sealed bottles of liquor. The walls are covered with nude art masterpieces and other landscape scenes. Every square inch is covered with gaming tables. They even have an orchestra that used to play forenoon, afternoon, and nights. When you throw Texan "whoops" and gunshots into the mix, it gets plumb rowdy.

Chad rides up to the large and imposing Drovers Cottage. A boy slips around the side of the building.

"Take you horse to the livery around back, mister?"

Chad steps from the saddle, pulls his saddlebags and his carpetbag off the horse.

"Yes, son. Here's a quarter. See that he gets oats." Chad flips the coin in the air, and it's snatched quickly by the boy.

"Yes, sir. Will do." He leads the horse away.

Chad stands at the foot of the stairway leading to the covered veranda that extends across the front of the Cottage. Through the front door, a porter rushes down the steps toward Chad. His pinstripe pants, black vest, white shirt, and pomaded hair parted in the middle take Chad by surprise.

"Yes, sir. Take your bag, sir. Follow me, please." The porter snatches at Chad's saddle and carpetbags.

"Whoa, feller." Chad tugs back on his bags. "What is this place?"

The porter pauses and stares at Chad in disbelief.

"This, sir, is The Drovers Cottage. It's the finest establishment west of St. Louis. We have over one hundred accommodations for extended stay, world-class dining rooms, and a laundry. We cater to owners, buyers, and solicitors for the cattle industry. May I ask what herd or concern you represent?"

"It's been at least two years since I pushed a herd to Abilene. Y'all weren't here then. There wasn't much here. Looks like a lot of change." Chad begins climbing the steps. The porter rushes onto the porch, heading for the front door.

"Yes, sir. There's been considerable change. Abilene is not the same wild town you experienced years ago. Law and order have been established. All drovers, wild cowboys, gamblers, dance hall girls, unsavory elements are required to stay south of the railroad. There is a mandatory 'no guns in town' law in effect. All handguns are surrendered when entering and returned when one leaves."

"How in the almighty do you get a cowboy to give up his sidearm?"

"Marshal 'Bear River' Tom Smith has had more than one altercation with recalcitrant, drunken cowboys and beaten them with his fists. No gunplay. Simple fisticuffs surprise and overcome the offenders."

"He must be some kind of man to whip his weight in wild, gun-totin, yee-hawin, drunk cowboys."

"Yes, sir. He was a mountain of a man and highly respected."

"Was?"

"Yes, sir. A farmer murdered him. The new marshal Bill Hickok is a different type, but not one to be messed with."

"Sounds like y'all have settled Abilene down quite a bit."

"We are a town of commerce, trade, and enterprise now. No longer a den of purveyors of sin, preying on intoxicated cowboys in their attempt to separate him and his money."

"Yep, that's the Abilene I remember."

"I've heard that farmers continue to push westward following the railroad. There are even stories of that dastardly barrier called barbed wire being strung over some prairie lands. The attempt is to keep cattle out and remove the threat of tick fever from local livestock." The porter holds the door for Chad to enter the lobby.

"Yeah. I read a newspaper article in Fort Worth about a barbed type of wire invented by a guy named John Gates. He's all about promoting it in Texas."

The porter ushers Chad into the Cottage.

Inside the door, Chad pauses. Before him is an elegant room with a round damask covered settee in the center. Additional couches are placed along the wall, matched with Queen Anne style chairs. Wall sconces provide light as well as does the large chandelier suspended in the middle of the room. Ten feet tall ceilings and a scattering of potted plants all create an inviting space.

Chad stands openmouthed at the appearance of the lobby.

"Yes, sir. It is quite breathtaking. I never tire of a first-time visitor's reaction. Let me check you in and see that your bags are taken to your room. You may want to go into the smoking den or the bar to relax."

Chad stammers, "The bar…that's fine."

"Very well, sir. What is your name? For our registration."

"Chadbourne Westerman."

"Very good. Please enjoy the bar, and pick up your key at the front desk when you are ready to go to your room. Good day." The porter hurries to the desk with Chad's bags.

Chad makes his way through batwing doors into the bar. Light is reflected off the dark mahogany walls onto tables arranged in the center of the room. He takes a seat at the closest table.

"What are you drinking, sir." The waiter appears beside the table.

"Bourbon, and leave the bottle," says Chad as he tries to take in all the changes. He becomes aware of a man standing beside him.

"Pardon me, sir." The man speaks to Chad. "It appears you are fresh off the range. Are you with a trail herd bossed by A.H. Pierce? He's called Shanghai Pierce."

Chad leans back in his chair to look at the stranger. The man wears a dove gray three-piece suit with a key chain draped from pocket to pocket across his vest. His boots are shiny black, and he sports a black Stetson with no sweat stains or creases. Brown eyes above a handlebar moustache stare at Chad.

"Who's askin'? Where can I get a set of duds like yours?" Chad scoots his chair back making it easier to reach his pistol.

He looks down at his dirty blue pullover shirt, leather vest, worn Levis, and stovepipe fringed chaps. He's aware of his scuffed brown boots and stained hat that lies on the table.

"Roger Austin, sir, at your disposal. There's a haberdasher in the Cottage next to the tonsorial parlor. A shave and bath may be in order." The man's eyes look Chad over closely.

Chad recalls the last bath he had was in the Arkansas River. "What's your interest in Shanghai Pierce?"

"I represent the cattle owners from Waco area. Mister Pierce is driving their herd to the railroad pens."

"You represent them? What does that mean?"

"I'm their lawyer."

"Why do they need a law-dog?"

"I'm here to make certain the business transaction with the buyers goes without incident and that the funds are transferred to their Austin, Texas, bank. I do object to your expression of *law-dog*."

"So the owners don't trust Shanghai?"

"Oh, no, on the contrary. They trust him implicitly. They've just heard too many stories about Abilene. Wild cowboys, wicked gamblers, and purveyors of perfidy."

"I see. Well, you better climb aboard your cayuse and ride down the trail to make sure ol' Shanghai ain't been led astray."

"You, sir, are joshing me, aren't you?"

Chad rises, puts his hat on, and walks toward the saloon door. He turns at the door.

"Yep. I'm joshin'. I don't think you could fork a horse for long. Good day, sir." He steps into the lobby, spots the sign for the tonsorial parlor, and moves that direction.

A barber's shave and a hot, steaming bath is just what I need. Then I'll find some new clothes.

The scent of Bay Rum aftershave proceeds Chad through the doorway onto the veranda of The Drovers Cottage. He looks at tables and chairs placed around the porch where men sit in conversations.

Chad moves toward a small group standing at the corner of the porch. All are dressed similarly in dark colored suits. None wear holsters or side arms. Most have drinks in their hands. He overhears an ongoing conversation.

"Yes, gentlemen, the eastern markets can't seem to get their fill of western beef. The meatpackers in Chicago and points east are clamoring for more shipments of cattle." A short man with a bowler hat speaks with authority. "Yes, sir. Got to make more deals and ship more beef."

"The railroad is making all the difference. We ship beef there and they ship everything imaginable from the factories and stores out here. East meets west along the railway." The man wearing a felt, flat-crowned hat looks around the group for acceptance and receives nods of approval. He stops at Chad.

"You, sir, have the appearance of a cattleman. Have you delivered a herd to Abilene?"

"I've just arrived. I'm not a cattleman although I've travelled with a herd that's approaching town. I'm a range detective."

"A Pinkerton?"

"Nope. Employed by a concern in Texas."

"You're a little north of your jurisdiction, detective. Aren't you?"

"Oh, my jurisdiction is flexible when I'm trailin' a killer."

"You're on the trail of a killer?"

"Yep. Ain't a one of you killed anybody lately, have you?"

With cautious looks and a nervous twitter of laughter, the group members shake their heads.

"Good, then I ain't after a one of you. My name's Chadbourne Westerman, I don't believe I got any of yours."

"Sorry, Mister Westerman," says the man wearing a black bowler hat. "That's Luke Short." Chad looks at the man with a straw boater. "Over there is Tom Hood and Lucius Martin." The men nod, they're wearing low crowned Stetsons. "Beside you is Artemus Gordon." He wears a felt hat with a tall crown. "I'm Alexander Heart."

"Howdy, men. What's that you were saying about the railroad?"

"I was saying that the railroad makes many things available out here that we never had before. This hotel wasn't here a few years ago. It's built to accommodate us cattle buyers so we can negotiate purchases with herd owners."

"So, this place is for cattle buyers and owners?" Chad looks around the group as they nod almost in unison.

"The town is north of the tracks, and the law keeps drovers and other riff raff on the other side of the tracks, the south side. Marshal Smith did a great job of maintaining order up until that sodbuster ambushed him. Now, Wild Bill Hickok is the new marshal and doing a fine job. He even backed down one of your fellow Texans, John Wesley Hardin."

"What about the sodbusters you were sayin' earlier? Oh, and Hardin ain't nothin' but a preacher's kid gone bad."

"Farmers are using the railroad to move onto the prairies. They see all this grassland out here and want nothing more than to fence it and farm it. It's going to mean the end of open range for your cattle drives." The felt hatted man gets confirming nods from the group.

"That means y'all will be out of business without cattle to buy."

"No. That means we will just move down the line further west and keep in front of the farmers."

"Well, men, you've been downright enlightening. I appreciate your conversation." Chad starts to step away from the group.

The short man with a straw boater hat stops him.

"You said you are a detective?"

"Yep." Chad turns toward the man.

"I was down at loading pen number two late yesterday and saw the strangest sight."

"Okay. What did you see?"

"It was getting close to dusk, and I thought I saw. Well, I can't be certain, but I thought I saw a nun wandering around the pens."

"How sure are you it was a nun?" Chad gives the man his full attention.

"Like I said, it was dusk, and sometimes your eyes play tricks on you at that time of day. I think it was a nun."

"Aw, Luke, there ain't no nuns in Abilene. Were you coming back from the Alamo on Cedar Street?" The felt hatted man laughs out loud as others from the group join him.

"I was stone cold sober and know what I saw, or think I saw."

"Loading pen number two, a nun, right?"

"Yes, sir, that's what I think."

Chad nods and turns leaving the group laughing to themselves. He quickly walks down the front steps and around to the livery in back.

17

LOADING PENS

"**K**EEP 'EM BUNCHED UP AND DON'T ALLOW NO stragglers." Angus rides up and down the herd directing the cowboys. "Keep pushin' them toward loadin' pen number three. Y'all see the three painted on that board ahead?"

"We see it, Boss," shouts Benjamin. "Keep at it, boys." The cowboys shout, slap their lariats against their chaps, whistle, and push the cows toward the pen beside the railroad tracks. The corral keeper swings the double gates wide open to allow cattle to fill the enclosure.

"Benjamin, get to the fence and sit atop it to get a head count. The buyer is sittin' up there right now. Sit beside him. I want to make sure the tally is right." Angus points toward the corral.

"Yes, Boss, on my way." Benjamin spurs out in front of the

plodding herd.

Angus shouts at a wrangler cowboy.

"Tell Russell to drive the horses to the corral over yonder." He points to a rail corral sitting apart from the holding pens. "Let him know I'll meet him at Drover's Cottage."

"Yes, Boss." The wrangler spins his horse around and gallops toward the remuda.

Benjamin reaches the holding pen, dismounts, and climbs to the top rail beside the buyer.

"Hello, young man." The buyer acknowledges Benjamin. "Y'all have a good-sized herd comin' in." The buyer wears a flannel shirt, Levis, scuffed boots, and a sweat stained felt hat.

"Yes, sir. We've pushed these beeves from the Hill Country of Texas to here."

"Quite an accomplishment. Yes, sir, quite an accomplishment. Much trouble along the way?"

"Ha, what trouble?" *River crossings, Bucky and Lamont killed, stampede, dead cattle, Indians, dirt, heat, rained on, sunburnt, but no troubles.*

"That's good to hear. Ready to get a count?"

"Good to go, sir. Here they come now." Cattle begin entering loading pen number three. Benjamin and the buyer watch the cowboys continue to whoop, holler, and flail their lariats as cattle stream past them. The next few hours are busy counting. Benjamin has his piggin' string out and ties a knot after he counts each fifty head of cattle.

"Well, Mister Tremain, Benjamin's count and mine match. Averaging your two-and-four-year-old, steers and cows, I'm authorized to purchase your twenty-four hundred and for-ty-five head of cattle at thirty dollar a head. I know that's a good price this season. Nobody can beat it. Plankinton and Armour Company pay the best for the best."

"I'm pleased at the price, Mister Short. You've got yourself a herd." Angus stands at the corral with his arms crossed over the top rail, watching the cattle mill around.

"I'll meet you in a couple of hours at Cattleman's Bank to finish the financials. We can transfer funds from my account to yours. You'll need money to pay off your drovers, and they'll have cash in hand. You'll need to arrange your letter of credit or a method to transport your funds back to Texas. That's your decision. Is there anything else you'll need?"

"I'm plannin' on takin' the train home. Can I make arrange-ments at Drovers for that?"

"Certainly. The Cottage caters to everything we need to make cattle purchasing go smooth."

"Do you know if a friend of mine, Chadbourne Westerman, is at Drovers?"

"Funny you mention Mister Westerman. We talked with him just yesterday. He introduced himself as a range detective tracking a killer."

"Yep. That's him. He's doin' just that."

"Well, well. He's staying at Drovers Cottage. He was very in-terested in something I mentioned seeing around the loading pens the other day."

"Cattle, drovers, what?"

"A nun."

"A what?"

"Nun. You know black hood and beads."

"I know. I know. Where did you see this nun?"

"It was dusk, and I saw the nun walking between the pens. Only briefly."

"Chad knows this?"

"Oh yes, he rushed away from our group after I told him. I believe he came to the pens to check things out."

"Let me talk with my crew, and I'll join you at the Cottage. If you happen to see Chadbourne, tell him I'm lookin' for him as well."

"I will Mister Tremain. I'll see you soon." The buyer jumps from the top rail and walks to his waiting buggy.

"Benjamin, gather the boys over at the loading master's building. I need to talk with y'all before cuttin' you loose."

"Yes, Boss, I'll round them up and get them there." Benjamin jumps from the top rail and mounts his horse. He rides out to round up the crew.

A nun. Here in Abilene. Chadbourne knows and is investigating. We'll get to the bottom of this real quick. Got to warn the boys about Abilene and find out who's takin' the train with me back to Texas. By gosh, a bath and bed are gonna feel good.

Angus' cowboys stand in a semi-circle around him beside the loading pen. He looks them over.

They were boys when we left the hill country. With what we've been through, they've growed up. I'd ride with them anywhere. Now, I got to get them home safe to their families.

"All right, listen up. I know y'all want to cut loose but pay attention."

"We want a real bath and shaves, Boss," replies Benjamin. "Some new clothes would be right fine as well."

"I know, I know, and I'm right there with you. What you have to understand is that this town is here to steal everything from you right down to your long-johns."

"We ain't got much to steal." A tow-headed cowboy says with a laugh. The other boys nod in agreement.

"Well, you ain't been paid yet neither, and it's the money in your pockets that the gamblers and whores sniff."

"You payin' us now, Boss?" A cowboy takes off his black hat and slaps it against his chaps.

"Directly. I'm headed to the bank to collect for the herd and will be at Cowtown Hotel lobby just a block north of the Alamo saloon on Cedar at noon. You'll be paid then."

"We'll go there and wait for you, Boss." Benjamin turns to lead the cowboys toward town.

"Boys, before you go, I need to know if any of you are goin' to ride the train back home? I'm fixin' on leavin' day after tomorrow by train and you're welcome to go with me. Only other way home is back the way we come."

The cowboys stop and look from one to another. A few heads nod, and Benjamin speaks for the bunch.

"Boss, we seen what's behind us, and would like to ride a train. We'll go with you."

"That's good news, boys. I'll be at the depot at eight o'clock in the morning and have tickets for you."

"Eight o'clock day after tomorrow, right?"

"Yep. You've got rooms waitin' for you at Merchants Hotel. Russell is already there waitin' on you. Three of you to a room, but the beds are big."

"Thanks, Boss," says Benjamin.

"If y'all are agreeable, I'll give you half of your earnings at noon and the other half when you board the train. Call it a savings account. It might remove temptation from cleanin' you out. It's all your money. You've earned it. What do you say about doin' this?"

The cowboys talk quietly among themselves.

Benjamin looks at Angus. "That'll be fine, Boss. We'll see you at the hotel at noon." They walk to their horses and mount.

Angus watches them ride toward town.

I'm right proud of them boys. Smart and level headed. They're growin' into fine men. I'll see they get home.

Angus mounts, and rides to the bank.

18

WRAPPING UP

CHAD SITS ON THE WIDE VERANDA OF DROVERS Cottage, gently moving in his rocking chair. His feet are crossed and resting on the porch rail. Taking a long drag on the thick pungent cigar he holds, he exhales well-defined rings of smoke upward. Two figures on horseback approach the Cottage.

"It's about time you two lonesome cusses drag yourselves into town."

"We had a herd to bring into town, sell it and the remuda, settle our drovers into a hotel, and collect our money. We ain't no so-called range detective that cavorts wherever he pleases." Angus and Russell turn their horses over to the livery boy.

Chad rises as Angus and Russell climb the steps onto the veranda porch.

"Drag your duds into the lobby and get registered. Then we'll have a drink in the bar." A porter holds the door open for the men. He takes the saddlebags from Angus and Russell.

"Give the porter your names, and let's go to the waterin' hole. I know the way."

"I imagine you found that first, Chadbourne." The two men follow Chad.

The three sit at a table in the corner of the bar.

"This is some place," says Russell looking around.

"Yep. It's some place, and you've only seen a bit of it," agrees Chad. "The dining room is huge, and the food is great. Anything you want. The railroad delivers everything."

"Our stay will be short. We're heading home day after to-morrow," says Angus.

"How about the drovers?"

"They're goin' with us. What about you, Chadbourne?"

"Got unfinished business that needs takin' care of before I leave."

"That reminds me, I was talkin' to the buyer, a Luke Short, about somethin' he saw around the loading pens," says Angus.

"Luke, sure, I know Luke. I bet he said somethin' about seein' a nun."

"You're right. What have you found out?"

The bartender steps to the table.

"Bring us a bottle of Old Forester bourbon and three glasses," says Chad.

"Very good, sir." The bartender goes to the bar and returns with their order.

Chad pulls the cork and pours drinks all around. Raising his glass, he says, "To another completed drive."

The three men drink, and Chad pours another round. "I've

been down to the loading pens for the past couple of evenings and not caught sight of a nun. I'm beginning to doubt what Luke says he saw."

"Do you think the nun is our killer?" questions Angus.

"I don't know what our nun is, but I suspect she ain't a nun. Beyond that, I need to question him or her."

"You let Russell and me go and get settled in, bathed, and shaved, and we'll go with you to find this hide-away nun." Angus stands. Russell rises, and they both move to the door.

"I'll be right here or on the porch waitin' for you," says Chad.

Angus and Russell shove open the bat-winged doors and step outside.

Chad turns and nurses his bourbon, as the doors swing open.

"I knew I'd find you here." Isaac walks into the bar.

"Well, well, well. You mean Abigail turned you loose?"

"She's in town, north of the tracks, looking for a house to rent, a church, and a minister."

Chad sits back and pushes his hat back on his head.

"She's movin' fast ain't she?"

"We've talked quite a bit on our way from the Arkansas River to Abilene. I think she has the right idea."

"You're givin' up your snake-oil peddlin'?"

"I've told you before…oh, hell. I give up. Yes, I'm selling my wagon and taking up pharmacy fulltime. I see you're drinking some of my friend George Brown's fine bourbon."

"Your friend?"

"Oh, yes. George Brown is a trained pharmacist like I am. He and his brother started J.T.S. Brown Distillery in Louisville, Kentucky."

"Well, I'll be. Another snake-oil salesman gone legitimate."

"I've not done anything illegal…oh, it serves no purpose arguing with you. George has taken the notion that sealing his bourbon in glass bottles keeps it from being spiked with other additives. He's got the right idea, and it seems to be well received."

"Spikin' elixirs. You got the corner on that. You thinkin' about opening a distillery?"

"Oh, no. I'm satisfied being a pharmacist. That is honest enough work for me."

"Lord knows you're ready for honest work."

"Chadbourne, I am fed up with your insinuations and accusations."

"Okay, easy, easy. It's just that it is so easy. You're sure about weddin' Abigail? You don't know a lot about her, do you?"

"I know what we've talked about." Isaac's frustration is apparent, and he feels threatened by Chad's questioning.

"You think you could slow things down and still hang on to her?"

"Why should I? That may be possible, but why? Do you know something I don't?"

"I just know that something good is worth investin' some time into before you pull a trigger."

"I see. Now I get philosophy from a range detective."

"Speakin' of detecting, we got a job to finish. You stickin' with me until it's done?"

"We'd agreed that Abilene was the extent of my servitude, but I do not like to leave a job undone. I'm still with you." Isaac feels torn between completing a job and removing himself from Chad's tormenting remarks.

"Good, I need you to meet me this evening at the loading

pens. I'm lookin' for our elusive nun."

"You mean the one who disappeared from us on the prairie?"

"I think it's the one and same."

"I'll be there."

"Where are you and Abigail staying?"

"White's Hotel in town."

"Same room?"

"Why must you always go and spoil something…I give up with you. No. We each have our own room. There is nothing unseemly happening. I will not impugn Abigail's dignity or chastity until we marry. Are you quite finished with your inane questioning?"

Chad smiles as he rises and walks toward the door.

"See you at the loading pens at dusk, lover boy." Shoving the doors open, he leaves.

Isaac stands watching his friend walk away. *Detestable, uncouth, uncultured, ignoramus, and barely tolerable. I don't know why I put up with him. I should leave Chadbourne to his own devises, but he asked for my help. What mess is he leading me into?*

Chad rides into town and stops in front of the millinery shop three doors down from the Cotillion Hall on Second Avenue. He ties his horse to the hitching rail and steps onto the boardwalk. Couples are strolling along the boardwalk as they window shop, stop and talk, and move through the hall. Chad walks a few feet and recognizes the couple coming towards him.

He tips his hat. "Isaac and Abigail, it's good to see you. Have you found a house yet?"

"Not yet, Mister Westerman, but I am surveying what is available," says Abigail. "I understand you continue to ask Isaac for assistance."

"Only for a short while longer. Did you enjoy the music at the Cotillion?"

"The orchestra played well," says Isaac. He tugs at Abigail's arm to keep walking.

Chad steps to the side and tips his hat. "Have a good evening." To Isaac as they pass he says, "See you later." Isaac nods.

Turning he watches the couple depart.

That is some girl. She lights out on her own, wrecks, attaches herself to us, enamors Isaac, and looks to settle in Abilene. Can she make Isaac a happy man?

Turning around, he almost collides with a tall man on the boardwalk.

"I beg your pardon, sir...Shanghai, you old dog."

"Chadbourne Westerman, you're a long way from Uvalde."

"Well, you're a long way out of Texas, too. Where you livin' now?"

"My brother and I have Rancho Grande on the Tres Palacios River in Wharton County. I've just brung a herd to Abilene."

"Angus Tremain, you remember Angus?"

"Sure do, he's a hard one to forget."

"He just brought a herd in as well. I came with him. I'm doin' some range detective work for clients down my direction."

"You sure are a long way off your range for detective work."

"I gotta go where the leads take me."

"I saw you talkin' with that gal a minute ago. She's some looker ain't she? Her red shoulder length hair fairly glimmers, those curves are all the right size and in the right places, that face is beautiful, and those dark ebony eyes can see right into your soul."

"Whoa, Shanghai I believe she's captivated you. She's with my friend Isaac Wisenheimer. He's a snak…pharmacist."

"I ain't captivated by nothin', just attracted. I was tryin' to get close to her. I believe I've seen her here in Abilene before."

"Her? Here? When? She work at one of the houses?"

"It was at least a year ago. Naw, she ain't a workin' girl. She was lookin' for someone, her dad. Don't remember all the details. Maybe I got her confused with someone else. Well, I gotta catch up with my boys down to the Alamo. I'll see you down the trail, Chadbourne."

"Always good to bump into you Shanghai. I'll be seein' you." The two separate and go opposite directions.

Abigail's been here before. Lookin' for her dad. Could she be the same person? What's she doin'? Why's she here? Need to talk with Isaac.

Chad turns and walks into the Cotillion Hall.

19

TERMINATION

THE FOUR MEN STAND IN THE GROWING DARKNESS. Dusk rapidly brings an end to the day. They congregate between two loading pens where cattle mill around, waiting to be loaded into cattle cars the next morning.

"Will the nun show up?" asks Isaac.

"I have no idea. What I do know is that if he or she does show, we'll be here to grab her," says Chad looking at the other men. "What we need to do is split up. Angus and Russell, cover the area around pens one and two. Isaac and I will handle three and four. We'll meet at four and all take a look at the horse corrals after that. Sound all right with that?"

"You do know that I don't work for you, don't you?" Angus looks at Chad. "I'll wander over there with Russell a piece." Angus moves toward his designated pens with Russell.

"That's mighty big of you, Angus," replies Chad. "I'm starting around pen three, I'll meet you in the middle after you circle four."

"You got it. On my way." Angus saunters off.

Chad and Isaac separate and begin their walk around the loading pens.

The sun disappears completely over the horizon, and darkness settles like a cloak around the pens. Chad stands still beside a fencepost, listening. The cattle make hearing clearly difficult.

There it is, another step coming my direction. I know Isaac is around the other side of the pen, so who is this? Listen. Listen. There it is again. Slow, almost creeping in my direction.

The moon slips from behind scurrying clouds and casts light on the area. Chad sees a figure moving stealthily toward him.

Closer, closer, just a little bit farther.

"Chad, you see anything? It's so dark out here, I cannot even see my hand in front of my face." Isaac shouts from across the pen.

The figure freezes, turns to look in Isaac's direction, and breaks into a run toward Chad.

Stepping from behind the post, Chad collides with the running figure. Grabbing, snatching, each tries to untangle from the collision.

Chad manages to get to his knees, pull his Colt, and press the barrel against the head of the prone figure.

"Don't wiggle, move, or sneeze. This iron will blow a hole through your head big enough to reach through."

The figure stops struggling and lies still.

"Isaac, call Angus and Russell. Get over here and bring a

193

lantern with you. I saw one hanging on the fence post earlier."

Chad hears Isaac shout out for the other men and comes running his direction.

Isaac runs up, stops, sits down the lantern, raises the chimney, pulls a Lucifer, and lights the wick. A pool of light cuts a hole in the darkness illuminating the area. He hangs the lantern from a bracket on the holding pen.

On the ground, with Chad's pistol pressed against it, lies a nun.

Angus and Russell rush into the circle of light.

"Well, I'll be a two-headed billy goat. It is a nun," says Russell. "Get her up. Don't keep her pinned on the ground, Chad."

"I'm not movin' this nun until I know something." He reaches over and yanks the hood from the nun's head. "Turn the wick up on the lantern."

Isaac increases the light.

Short hair is visible on the nun's head.

"Did she cut her hair?" asks Isaac, surprised by the sight.

"She or he, ain't sure yet," answers Chad. "Stand up real slow and easy. My finger can snap this trigger real quick." Chad rises to allow the nun to stand.

Slowly, the figure rises.

"Shuck out of that robe and be quick about it," Chad orders.

"You want a nun to stand neckked out here?" Angus looks shocked.

"I'm fairly convinced it ain't no nun, Angus."

Slowly, the figure unties the beaded belt wrapped around her waist, slides the cloak off her shoulders, and drops it to the ground.

"Glory be, it ain't a she. It's a he." Angus pushes his hat back on his head.

Standing before them is a short man, wearing a dirty white pullover shirt, worn Levis, and scuffed up brown mule eared boots.

"Why?" asks Chad.

"I had to. I'm on the dodge from U.S. Marshals and Pinkertons."

"You still ain't answered my question 'Why'."

"A bank robbery in Austin. Didn't get much. Most of it left with my brother when they caught up with us in Waco. He died. I ran. Snatched these nun clothes from a wash line at a church outside Dallas. Been running ever since."

"Why not dump them in the Territory or here in Abilene?" Chad keeps his pistol on the man.

"Couldn't be sure if I was bein' followed or if the marshal here was telegraphed and waitin' for me to turn up."

"Why'd you stalk me out on the prairie? That was you paralleling me out there, wasn't it?"

"It was. I'd come up over a rise and spotted you. I figured you saw me so turnin' away would only bring you on the run. I decided to keep out of range and ride a while, then slip away again."

"What do we do with him now, Chad?" Isaac asks.

"Turn him over to Hickok to hold for a U.S. Marshal. Grab my piggin' string off my saddle horn and tie him up."

Isaac walks to the horses and finds the short length of rope. He returns and hands it to Russell who ties up their captive.

"Let's get him to jail." Chad holsters his pistol as Angus and Russell lead the man over to the horses.

"You think he's the killer?" asks Isaac.

"Don't know. Don't see any reason for him killin' anybody

but will have to find out more at the jail."

"I left the lantern lit, I better put it out." Isaac moves to walk back to the pen.

Chad stops him. "Go ahead, I'll get it. You keep up with Angus."

Reaching the pens, Chad reaches up to the lantern, raises the chimney, and starts to blow out the flame.

He stops.

He feels a steel blade press against his throat. A hand presses hard against his back and a voice whispers in his ear.

"You think you're so smart, don't you?"

Chad is motionless, not moving a muscle. He recognizes the voice.

"Can't say that." Chad knows it's a bowie knife pressing against his windpipe. "Don't think I'm too smart standing here with a knife on me."

"You've been trying to figure out who killed the cowboys, and you think you've done it, don't you?"

"Can't say that for a fact. But think you've got something to do with it."

"Ha. Besides this knife. Why me?"

"I think it's took someone close to us. Someone the boys trusted. Somebody who knew when the boys went places."

"Anything else?" The knife presses harder against Chad's throat.

"I'd like to know why before you kill me too."

"You would, would you? I knew Isaac would lead me to you. How about if someone you loved was butchered and left hacked to pieces by cowboys he trusted. Would that be reason enough?"

"Seems that happened to the boys you've killed."

"They only reminded me of those who killed my father, stole his money, and destroyed my life. Cowboys, miserable cowboys that he trusted."

"Killin' more don't bring him back."

A shrill hysterical laugh shocks Chad.

"No, it doesn't, but it eases the mind. Now, it's your turn to die, cowboy." The knife pressure increases, and Chad feels a warm trickle of blood ooze down his neck.

One swift yank and I'm done. Chad steels himself for the end.

The cocking of a pistol hammer shatters the night.

"Put the knife down, Abigail." Isaac presses the pistol against her back as he steps into the pool of light.

There's a slight release of pressure on the knife. Chad catches a breath.

"You won't shoot me, Isaac. You love me."

"I love the woman who isn't a monster that butchers young boys."

"They needed to die, Isaac. They were just like those who killed my father."

"They weren't the same ones. You murdered them."

"You men are so easily manipulated. They saw me, trusted me, and did what I wanted. Just like you."

"Put the knife down, Abigail."

"One quick yank and Chad's head is severed from his body. I've done it so many times before. It's quite easy."

"You won't see the end. This Colt will blow a hole through you big enough to see tomorrow. What will you prove by doing it?"

"It's not about proving anything. It's about justice."

"Justice for your long dead father? Is this what he would want?"

"It's what I want. You just don't see that, do you." The knife pressure decreases and lifts a little from Chad's neck.

"Chad didn't do anything to your father. All he did was befriend you, and this is how you repay him?"

"If I don't stop him, he'll turn me in to the law."

"You're already found out; don't you see that?"

"Yes, but you won't turn me in. You love me."

"Abigail, think very carefully, I'm standing here with a cocked pistol ready to shoot you. Kill you, if you continue to harm Chad. It's over. Everything is over. Drop the knife."

"You are threatening me, Isaac? You would do that to me?"

"Not threatening. Promising. Put the knife down."

Abigail suddenly pulls the knife away from Chad, spins around, and raises it over her head preparing to plunge it into Isaac.

The Colt revolver fires, the sound explodes in the quiet night.

Abigail hurls backwards and sprawls on the ground in front of Isaac.

Chad grabs his neck feeling for a slash.

Isaac stands motionless for a moment, then throws aside the pistol, and drops to his knees beside Abigail. He watches the blood blossom across the front of her chest. She coughs, gags, and coughs again. He picks up her head and cradles it in his lap.

"Why, why, why did you make me do this?"

"It had to end this way," she whispers through bloody bubbles.

"You made me do this. I love you."

"You men are so easy. Any boy brought me a saddled horse when I asked and kept it our secret. I sent you off to work the herd or be with Chad. As long as I kept to the cattle trail, my horses' tracks were untraceable. I'm sorry for the Indian I killed. He was in the wrong place at the wrong time." Abigail slowly exhales and lies still.

Chad kneels on the other side of Abigail.

"I killed her, Chad."

"You had to, Isaac, or else she'd have killed me." He rubs his neck feeling the shallow weeping wound and raised welt from the knife blade.

Isaac brushes hair from Abigail's face and runs his hand along her cheek.

"Did she love me, Chad?"

"I can't answer that Isaac. I don't know."

"She's our killer?"

"Yes. She probably caught on to us at the gatherings and stalked us from there."

"Why?"

"Pain, hurt, loss at her father's murder. It turned her bitter, and bitterness changed to hatred and revenge. I believe it was eatin' her up."

"All the boys lives. She took them."

"Yes. I'm not sure, probably even the three down in south Texas. But from Fredericksburg to here, I believe she's responsible."

"So much hate, so much hurt."

"Shanghai Pierce said he's seen her in Abilene before. I don't think ours is the first drive she stalked."

Isaac inhales deeply and exhales a shuddering sigh. He breaks into gasping sobs and drops across Abigail's body. Chad reaches over and pats his back, letting him cry.

20

HOME BOUND

CHAD SITS ON HIS HORSE BESIDE THE LOADING PENS, watching cattle being prodded up the chutes into the cattle cars. It's been a week since he'd said goodbye to Angus, Russell, and the drovers as they boarded their railroad coach. He looks over at the chuckwagon beside him.

"Manolito, why didn't you sell your wagon and take the train home?"

"*Señor* Chad, my wagon is my business. I cannot sell my business. Besides why would I want to ride that noisy thing all the way to *Tejas*?"

"It's a long way back to Texas, mind if I ride along with you?"

"Oh no, *señor*, I would like the company. We can have *muy mas* biscuits, *si*?"

"Coffee and biscuits, *amigo*."

"*Si, es muy bueno.*"

Chad watches another rider leave town and approach the pens.

"Isaac, what are you doing out here?"

"Hello, Chad. *Buenos dias*, Manolito. I'm as well as I can expect to be and better than I deserve."

"*Hola, señor* Isaac. I am sorry about *señorita* Abigail." Manolito's face shows sadness.

"Me too, Manolito. Me too."

"I heard the mortician gave her a fine funeral." Chad shifts uncomfortably on his saddle.

"Yes, he did a fine job," answers Isaac. "It's over now."

"Where's your wagon, your elixirs, your snake-oil?"

"I've told you until I am almost blue in the face, I don't sell snake…oh hell. What's the use? I sold the entire rig, elixirs and all."

"What are you fixin' to do now?"

"Not sure. Wondered if I could travel along with you until I sort things out."

"You think you're ready to travel? Healin' the heart takes a while."

"I am as ready as I'll ever be. Staying here does not help."

"Manolito and I are bound for Texas. You willin' to go back down the Trail?"

"I came up the Chisholm Trail. I imagine I can return the same way. May help me remember some good times and forget Abilene."

"We've got to stop at Red River Station and pick up the boots from Justin's. I told Angus and the boys I'd fetch them home for 'em."

"Stopping in Red River Station will be fine. I could do with another meal at Mollie Love's place. No reflection on your meals, Manolito. It's just that she is nicer to look at than you are."

"*No problemo, señor* Isaac. We will eat *frijoles*, biscuits, and beefs on the prairie, *si*?"

"Okay, I guess we're Texas bound. Lead out Manolito, we've got plains and rivers to cross." Chad motions forward.

Manolito turns his chuckwagon south, snaps the reins over the mules' backs, and rolls out. Isaac rides on one side of the wagon, and Chad is on the other.

Three for Texas, just down the trail a ways. Chad adjusts his hat.

AFTERWORD

I hope you enjoyed this novella. If you did, I would be very grateful if you would write a customer review. Independent Authors don't have the resources of the publishing houses. We rely on our readers to promote our books by posting reviews.

Please locate the book on Amazon.com. Type my name in the search bar. My books should appear. Click on the book title. Near the bottom of the page, just below the "More About the Author" section, you will see a Customer Review area. Please click the 'Write a customer review' button and provide your feedback on the book. It will be greatly appreciated.

William A. Burgdorf

For more information about Dr. Wm. A. Burgdorf and his books, you may want to visit the author's websites:

www.waburgdorf.com

Adventures of Bocephus & Kate
learningaboutabunch.wordpress.com

and email: DrBilly@waburgdorf.com.

REPENTANCE

By

WM. A. BURGDORF

1

STRUNG OUT

THE HOT SUN BEAT DOWN ON THE FARMER. HE STOPS, reaches in the back pocket of his overalls, and pulls out a red bandana. Shaking it open, he wipes his brow, then his head, sopping up the sweat.

Stretched that barbed wire at least a hundred yards, dug the post holes, set the poles, and rolled out the wire. I'm going to protect my crops and keep cattle from crashing through this year. He hears a metallic clipping sound behind him.

"What do you think you're doing?" He shouts at a cowboy sitting on his horse with wire cutters in his hand. A single strand of wire is still attached to a pole the farmer set in the ground earlier.

The cowboy motions the farmer closer to the barbed wire with the pistol in his hand. The farmer moves next to the wire.

Leaning over in the saddle, the cowboy cuts the wire. The barbed wire quickly begins to roll up on itself as it seeks to return to its original bundle shape.

The farmer lets out a scream as the barbed wire wraps around him. He stands firm momentarily, then his foot slips and he is rolled up into the bundle. Screaming, shouting, and cussing, the barbs cut and shred his clothes and skin. Blood begins flowing and colors the ground as the farmer is rolled along.

The cowboy drops the wire cutters in his saddlebags and rides away. His cattle are bunched up over the hill waiting to move.

Chadbourne Westerman sits at the window table in Mollie Love's Restaurant in Red River Station finishing his coffee and apple pie. Across the table, Isaac Wisenheimer shakes the newspaper he holds in front of him to turn a page.

"It says here," Isaac points at the paper. "A Joseph Glidden of DeKalb, Illinois, has the patent for fencing materials of barbs wrapped around a single strand of wire. A Henry Bradley Sanborn is in San Antonio demonstrating how this 'barbed wire' can restrain longhorn cattle. Now that's something I'd like to see."

"We were down in San Antonio after that drive we made to Abilene back in '70," replies Chad.

"Yes, but we're back here in Red River Station again. I don't know why you had to take the job of U.S. Deputy Marshal anyway. We were doing just fine moving from ranch to ranch helping solve problems."

"Yep. Needed something more stable than range detective and north Texas needed a marshal. So, here we are. What are you complaining about, you've always liked Mollie's place?"

"Oh, I like it here all right especially since most the dirty, noisy herds have drifted west of here for crossing the Red River. I understand Dodge City, Kansas, is as bad as Abilene used to be."

"It's an end-of-the-trail-town and bound to be kind of lively when the herds arrive."

"Do you have any hankering to go back up the trail, the Western Trail?"

"Nope. Done all that drivin' I hanker to do. I'm set just keepin' an eye on northeast Texas and the Territory."

"Seems kind of limiting to me, but it's your job. Besides, I'm just along for the adventure." Isaac sits back and laughs aloud. "Yep, the adventure. That's what I am seeking."

Chad motions the waiter for more coffee and watches as the man fills his cup.

It's been a few years since Abilene and the trail drive. Manolito, our Mexican cook, Isaac, and I came back down the Chisholm Trail, picked up the drovers' new boots in Red River Station from Justin's, and delivered them to the boys in San Antonio. We rambled around central Texas investigating cattle problems for a couple of years. Then I met up with the U.S. Marshal in Austin and took him up on being a deputy. It's a good life.

The front door bursts open and a teenager runs into Mollie's. He looks around and runs over to Chad.

"Marshal, come quick. Some farmers brought a sodbuster in to the doctor."

"So, what's that got to do with me?"

"He's rolled up in barbed wire and mumblin' something about cowboys cuttin' his wire."

Chad kicks his chair back as he rises and rushes for the door. Isaac throws down his newspaper and is right behind.

ABOUT THE AUTHOR

WILLIAM BURGDORF leverages a lifetime of experiences into his stories accumulated from being born along the mighty Ohio River in southern Indiana, raised in the wide, wild desert vistas of Arizona, having lived in lake-strewn Michigan, as well as the hills and hollows of Tennessee, and now in his piney woods home in East Texas. His love of, and a double major in, history along with his successful career as an adult educator prepared him to become a masterful storyteller of historical fiction. His careful attention to exacting details, colorful and memorable characters, descriptive locales, and articulate dialogue weave together stories that engage and enthrall.

"My goal is to provide a story that captures your imagination and is remembered. At the end of the day, I desire to be regarded as a good 'storyteller.'

Website: www.waburgdorf.com
Facebook: www.facebook.com/william.burgdorf